CAPE COD
SURPRISE

ALSO BY
CAROL NEWMAN CRONIN

Oliver's Surprise

CRITICAL ACCLAIM FOR
OLIVER'S SURPRISE

"The best historical fiction combines good research with good storytelling, and *Oliver's Surprise* has it all. Carol Newman Cronin writes with authority about the sea and her home in Rhode Island, and her thorough investigation of the Hurricane of '38 shines through. Chock full of adventure, history, sailing, time travel, a likeable protagonist, *Oliver's Surprise* is about as much fun as you can have without actually being on board a boat!"

–JAMES L. NELSON, AUTHOR OF THE *REVOLUTION AT SEA SAGA* AND *GEORGE WASHINGTON'S SECRET NAVY*

"When our children were toddling, my wife's wish for them was confidence. But as they grew into teens what she wanted most for them was perspective. *Oliver's Surprise* is a fetching tale about a kid who through an uncommon set of travels gains just that kind of perspective—the kind that opens a curiosity about our own origins, the kind that places values from the past in our contemporary life, the kind that steers us toward our better selves. All this, and schooners, too."

–TIM MURPHY, EDITOR-AT-LARGE
CRUISING WORLD

"...an engaging tale woven by one of sailing's modern-day racing stars... a pleasant time-travel adventure for all ages."

–ELAINE DICKINSON, MANAGING EDITOR
BOATUS MAGAZINE

"A boy, a boat, and a bump on the head... the nautical tale is a treasure chest of surprises."

–*The Jamestown Press*

"For a kid smitten with the sea, an old schooner is the ideal vehicle for going back in time. Through young Oliver's eyes, Carol Newman Cronin offers a view of life along the 1930's Jamestown waterfront, just before the storm changed it forever. Above all, *Oliver's Surprise* reminds us of the connectedness of family and friends through generations."

–John Burnham, Editorial Director
Boats.com and *Yachtworld.com*

"*Oliver's Surprise* is about the past coming alive, how death and loss experienced in the moment are so much more acute than what the history books describe."

–Chris Abouzeid, author of *Anatopsis*

"I sat down to read *Oliver's Surprise* in California and was immediately transported to Jamestown and Narragansett Bay. This charming story—with lovely illustrations— captures two different eras in a very special place."

–Pease Glaser, *Olympic Silver Medalist*

"*Oliver's Surprise* is a wonderful young adult adventure story. The writing is fast-paced and filled with strong verbs and nautical terms. It reminds me of the *Wizard of Oz, Back to the Future,* and *Tom Sawyer/Huckleberry Finn* all rolled into one. Well done!"

–Paula Margulies, author of *Coyote Heart*

CAPE COD SURPRISE

Oliver Matches Wits with Hurricane Carol

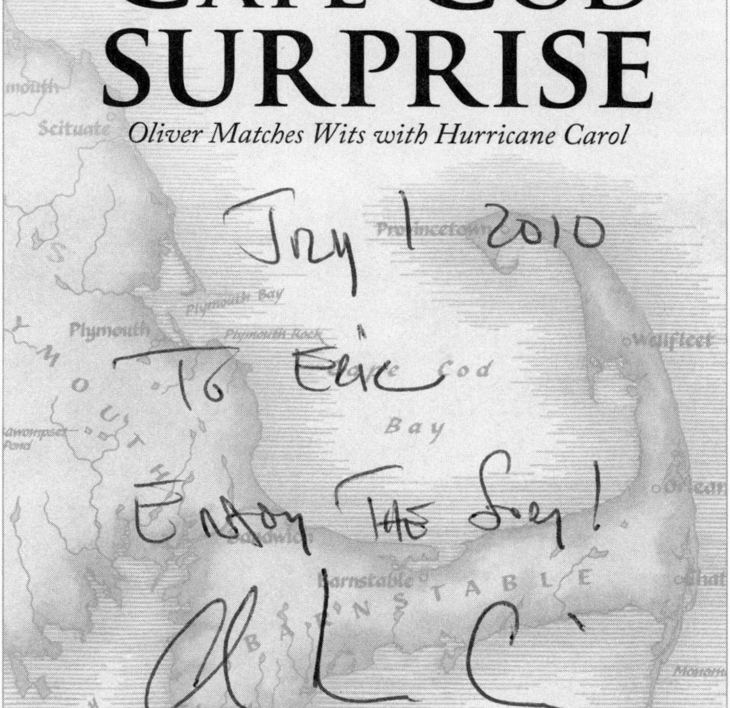

July 1 2010

To Eric

Enjoy The Story!

CAROL NEWMAN CRONIN

ILLUSTRATED BY
LAURIE ANN CRONIN

GEMMA
Boston

First published by GemmaMedia in 2010.

GemmaMedia
230 Commercial Street
Boston MA 02109 USA
617 938 9833
www.gemmamedia.com

Printed in the United States of America

14 13 12 11 10   1 2 3 4 5

ISBN: 978-1-934848-47-0

Library of Congress Control Number: 2010929174

Book design by Live Wire.
www.livewirepress.com

To The Others

Tessa • Celeste

Sam • Lydia

"Find yourselves within"

WANDERER'S SONG

A wind's in the heart of me, a fire's in my heels,
I am tired of brick and stone and rumbling wagon-wheels;
I hunger for the sea's edge, the limit of the land,
Where the wild old Atlantic is shouting on the sand.

Oh I'll be going, leaving the noises of the street,
To where a lifting foresail-foot is yanking at the sheet;
To a windy, tossing anchorage where yawls and ketches ride,
Oh I'll be going, going, until I meet the tide.

And first I'll hear the sea-wind, the mewing of the gulls,
The clucking, sucking of the sea about the rusty hulls,
The songs at the capstan at the hooker warping out,
And then the heart of me'll know I'm there or thereabout.

Oh I am sick of brick and stone, the heart of me is sick,
For windy green, unquiet sea, the realm of Moby Dick;
And I'll be going, going, from the roaring of the wheels,
For a wind's in the heart of me, a fire's in my heels.

–John Masefield

COMPANIONWAY *An opening that provides access between deck and cabin, usually protected with a sliding hatch.*

1

THE DIESEL RUMBLED TO LIFE beneath Oliver's bare feet—oh boy, that'd bring her running. They hadn't even left the dock this morning when Mrs. Haverford announced Rule Number One: "We will travel by sail this week, using the new engine only for emergencies."

Sure enough she popped up out of the cabin like a jack in the box, holding her perfect hair so the breeze didn't mess with it. But she'd found something else to grouse about.

"Cap'n Buck! We're out of water."

Buck lifted one hand off the wheel just long enough to slide a fresh peppermint into his mouth.

"It's just 'Buck,'" he told her. "No need to be calling me captain."

He'd been steering all day, eyes roaming over sun-sparkled water like he was daydreaming. Only the wake, straight as a highway, proved how well he was handling Surprise. They'd made great time on the sail up Buzzards Bay, and it sure wasn't from Mrs. H popping up on deck every five minutes. Never mind her useless son Greg—he'd spent the entire day staring down at a tiny MP3 player, white earphone wires dangling.

Mrs. Haverford pressed her lips together. "We'll discuss your title another time. Right now I need to wash up the lunch dishes, and nothing is flowing out of the faucet."

"We can't be out of water already—I just filled the tank this morning." Buck's eyes left the narrow channel of water ahead long enough to glance over at Oliver. "Could you take a look?"

Hitching up his cargo shorts, Oliver followed Mrs. H down the steep ladder into a cabin that reeked of new foam. Six cushions, blue with red piping, had been tucked into place that morning. Mrs. H swatted a crease out of the port settee on her way forward.

Above the settee, a battered canvas duffle waited in his bunk. Mom had packed for him, but he didn't really care what she'd stuffed inside that old blue bag of hers. Tonight he'd sleep head to toe with the captain of Surprise, just like a real ship's boy...that's if he could sleep.

The galley stretched across the forward end of the cabin—short counter, shiny stove, sink full of dishes. Mrs. H spun the hot water tap all the way open.

"All the money I spent to rebuild this schooner, you'd think the darn faucet would work." A pump whined, but no water came out. "See?"

"I'll check the tank."

Oliver lifted up the center floorboard—and gasped. The bilge shone with water! He couldn't even see the tank, but it must've sprung a leak.

So why hadn't the emergency pump come on?

The top switch on the electrical panel had been switched off, that's why. As soon as Oliver flipped it back to "auto," a deep gurgle began to pump their fresh water overboard.

Too weird–

A loud snicker from the starboard side of the cabin startled him. Greg Haverford lay in the bunk opposite Oliver's, knees up, nibbling the side of a thumb with his perfect teeth. He'd come below as soon as the waves had flattened out, and now he pulled the headphones out of his MP3 player and held the shiny rectangle up to his left ear. Tinny cymbals crashed, loud enough to hear across the cabin.

Mrs. H had invited Oliver along this week to have another "young person" aboard, but he and Greg would never be friends. It wasn't the four year age difference—Oliver had two buddies at home who would be seniors this fall. And it wasn't Greg's all-black sneakers, jeans, and T-shirt, or the two silver hoops spearing his left earlobe. It was his attitude. The guy even trash-talked his own mother.

And he was still snickering.

Back on deck, Oliver told Buck what he'd found—everything except for Greg's suspicious giggle.

"Damn." Buck's blond ponytail flicked back and forth as he shook his head. "We'll have to fill up again in Woods Hole."

He spun the wheel hard to port, swinging the bowsprit over a huge rock on the shore. Sails luffed overhead, then filled again as the schooner settled in on the other tack.

Too bad—now Oliver would have to wait even longer to check out Hadley's Harbor. Cap'n Eli had called this place the safest spot to be during a hurricane, which seemed impossible—how could anything be safer than dry land? Now that Oliver saw the two tan rocks guarding their narrow channel like a pair of unfinished gargoyles, it all made sense. Boats hidden inside showed only their masts, a white and silver forest poking up behind the brambles of the nearest island.

And with no engine, Eli must've sailed Surprise in and

out, threading her between those rocks! Now *that* seemed impossible.

Mrs. H popped out of the cabin again, grabbing onto the edge of the companionway to steady herself against Buck's sharp turn.

"What are you doing?" she asked him.

"Heading for Woods Hole to refill the tank. No supplies in Hadley's."

"That will delay our arrival."

Buck shrugged. "Can't do much without water."

"Cap'n Eli ran this boat for forty years and all he drank was rainwater." Mrs. Haverford's sharp gaze swiveled to the left, homing in on Oliver. "What do you think, young man? What would my father have done?"

In her father's day, Surprise didn't have a flush toilet.

It was just so hard to believe she was related to the jolly Eli, who'd ended every sea story with a wink. But she had made it possible for her father to die happy—by promising to rebuild his beloved schooner.

"No response, Oliver?" Buck smiled, his voice just carrying over the deep throb of diesel. "Then couldja get the jib down, please?"

Glaring at both of them, Mrs. H stomped down the companionway ladder again.

Oliver padded forward, the new wood deck warm underfoot from the afternoon sun. Up next to the foremast, a row of lines stretched down to the port rail. Untying the line marked "jib," Oliver let the sail collapse onto the deck and furled it against the boom.

Up here in the bow, away from the bickering and the tinny cymbals and the throb of diesel, he could hear water gurgling against the hull. Easy to imagine he was helping Cap'n Eli deliver a cargo of lumber. Or lobsters. Or stinky guano.

Surprise always seemed to take him on adventures. Last year she'd even taken him back in time, to 1938 and the big hurricane. Though lately he'd been wondering if that had been just a totally awesome dream.

Only thing was, all his memories lined up perfectly with Eli's stories.

How could he explain that, if it was all just a dream?

NUN *An unlighted, pointy-topped red buoy that is left on the starboard (right hand) side when returning to harbor. Shorthand for this navigation rule is "Red, Right, Returning."*

2

BACK IN THE COCKPIT, OLIVER hovered just behind Buck. Surprise was headed east again, nosing into the narrow channel of Woods Hole Passage. He'd heard the tide ran hard here between the southwest elbow of Cape Cod and the Elizabeth Islands, but—wow! The water swirled against them, flowing back out to Buzzards Bay as if rushing downhill. Rocks, buoys, and lobster pots all streamed a wake of their own, like when the waves ran out around Oliver's ankles at the beach. But this fast-moving water would knock him right off his—

"Oh no you don't!" Buck spun the helm hard to starboard.

Just off the bow, the biggest red buoy he'd ever seen dodged in their direction. Thanks to Buck's quick reaction, they missed it by two feet.

"Some tide." Oliver's voice cracked. The buoy danced away again, allowing the dory towing behind Surprise to clear it too.

"Current," Buck corrected. "Tide goes up and down."

On tiptoe, Oliver could just see the electronic chart over

Buck's shoulder. A squiggly red line showed where they'd been already, including the U-turn outside Hadley's. The black arrowhead marked Surprise's position right now, smack in the middle of a wide stripe of channel—so safe and obvious on the shiny screen.

"We gonna make it?"

"Oh we'll make it, thanks to the diesel." Buck tapped the throttle forward, increasing the rumble underfoot. "Cap'n Eli would've anchored till the current turned fair. With the engine, we're actually safer going through against it."

"Why?"

"Because we don't have to go as fast to maintain steerage. A rudder only works if there's water flowing over it."

Oliver didn't get it, but he didn't want to distract Buck with any more questions.

They passed right by a man-made heap of dark granite blocks guarding the middle of the pass. On the small island to port, a family had gathered for a late afternoon picnic—so close he could almost smell the onions in the potato salad. When the dark-haired girl waved Oliver could barely wave back, he was concentrating so hard on keeping Surprise away from the rocks between them.

The channel narrowed between the island and another huge buoy. The water swirled and eddied, and soon they were running in place—the current's speed matched theirs. Buck pushed the throttle forward another notch and they crept forward again, the beach and rocks inching past. This was taking forever, and they'd only gone half a mile.

Finally the island sloped away to port, revealing a harbor filled with boats—as many as his mom's entire boatyard. On the far shore sprawled a town of large brick buildings and even larger ships.

Another tumble of granite blocks slid by, topped by a checkered red and white square. Grassy Island, the chart

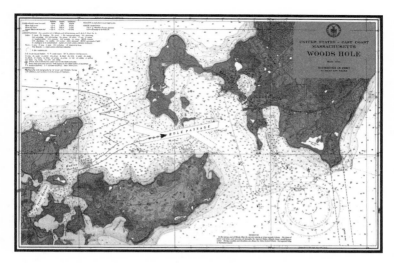

said—and not a blade of green in sight.

Just beyond it, Buck pointed to a lonely tip of seaweedy rock.

"Nine years ago I cut this corner too close and ran right up on that bad boy," he told Oliver. "Almost sank. Gotta be extra careful around here."

He gave the rock a wide berth in his curve around to port, the forgotten sails slatting across overhead onto the other tack. Ahead squatted the biggest squarest dock Oliver had ever seen. Two blue ships stood bow to bow, as tall as the town.

"Cap'n Buck! Would you kindly tell me what we are doing?" Mrs. Haverford popped up into the companionway again, her voice loud enough to be heard by everyone ashore.

"We're gonna tie up at the town dock and get some water," Buck told her. "Then we'll head back to Hadley's. Oliver, could you drop the foresail?"

Heading forward again, Oliver remembered the only injury recorded in Cap'n Eli's entire log:

> FORESAIL CAME DOWN TOO FAST AND BANGED UP MY
> HAND. LIZA WRAPPED IT IN A GASKET. FRESH BLUEFISH
> FOR DINNER.

He knew a gasket was what Mom would call a sail tie, and he knew what to do with it—tie the foresail up into a neat sausage that the wind couldn't grab. But who was Liza? The only female name in the whole book, besides the other schooners.

Last winter, while Surprise was rebuilt inside his mom's biggest shed, Cap'n Eli's logbook had been stored in the boatyard office. One day after school Oliver had pulled it off the shelf, piecing together the fat scrawl to learn everything he could about moving cargo by sail. He'd gone over the words so many times since then, he knew most of it by heart.

So Oliver felt like he'd already sailed into Woods Hole harbor, had already curved around past the large white ship with a forest of antennas and a huge dome up top. Except for the rumble of diesel, he could've been living through one of Eli's stories.

The town dock stuck out into the far corner of the harbor. Two red and white fishing boats filled up the far side, but the upwind face of the wood pier was empty.

"Time to get the main down," Buck called.

The sail piled itself neatly on top of the wide boom. All Oliver had to do was toss a couple of gaskets around it.

"Why not overnight in this nice harbor?" Mrs. H asked. "We don't have to adhere exactly to our itinerary."

"They're calling for a southeast blow late tonight, and that's a bad direction here." Buck patted the top of the wheel. "I'd hate to lose Surprise on her second maiden voyage."

Oliver climbed down off the cabin top. "Want me to rig some dock lines?"

"That sounds like something Greg could help with," Mrs. H said. "Greg, honey!" she called below. "Could you come up here, please?"

When her son's shaggy dark head appeared in the companionway, Mrs. Haverford stepped up into the cockpit.

Buck drew a deep breath. "We seem to be out of water."

Greg's eyes stayed on the small screen in his hand.

"So we're going into the town dock to refill. If you could–"

"Cool! So I can, like, get off?" Greg scrambled one-handed up the rest of the ladder.

"We're just getting water, not going ashore," Buck said. "Could you help Oliver, please? We'll need two fenders and–"

"Okay, okay." Stumbling up into the cockpit, Greg slid the MP3 player into his front pocket—but it missed. After one bounce off the cockpit seat and a second off the floor, it disappeared down through the scupper that drained water overboard.

"Shoot—where'd it go?"

"Swimming." Buck covered up his laugh with a short cough.

"Jeez! Mom–"

"That's okay, honey—we'll just get you another one. Listen to Cap'n Buck."

Greg's dark eyes darted around the schooner. "So where's the stuff?"

"In the lazarette." Still smiling, Buck throttled back to idle.

"The laz-er-what?"

"Lazarette," Mrs. H repeated, waving her pink nails aft toward the hatch that Oliver had just opened. "The word comes from the Italian, lazeretto. It once meant a place to quarantine–"

"Enough of the word lessons already." Greg rolled his eyes. "This is supposed to be a vacation, remember?"

"Fenders and docklines on the starboard side, please." Buck's voice tightened. "Quick now!"

Grabbing a thick white line and one of the gi-normous fenders (five feet tall, and almost as big around as he was), Oliver bumped up to the bow. The loop in the dockline fit perfectly around a large cleat, and he tied the fender off to the lifeline about ten feet back.

"Farther aft." Buck pointed almost halfway back to the stern. "Where she'll hit the dock first."

Surprise coasted into the narrow piece of water between the bow of the large white ship and the town dock. Just before the bowsprit touched a square brick building, Buck spun the wheel counterclockwise as far as it would go and gunned the throttle. Surprise turned to port, almost in her own length. Even Eli couldn't have done that under sail.

Bow out and parallel to the dock again, they crept forward, still twenty feet away.

I can't jump that far, Oliver thought. Buck's misjudged it...

But the wind did the rest, blowing the schooner toward the tar-oozing pilings.

"Toss her here, son." A man dressed in a fisherman's orange bibs looped two hitches around a thick piling, then ambled aft to grab the spring line from Mrs. H.

Buck reversed against the lines, squashing fenders between pilings and black hull. The dory wasn't so lucky—it bounced hard before Buck could pull the small boat up along the outside of Surprise.

"Mom, can I go get my new iPod now?" Greg still held a limp tail of stern line away from his body, as if it were an unpredictable snake.

"How long do you plan to be here, Cap'n Buck?" Mrs. H asked.

"Twenty minutes or so. I'd really prefer—"

"We'll both go," she decided. "Oliver can stay and help. I'll just change into nicer clothes—otherwise everyone will think I'm part of the crew."

Greg rolled his eyes again—he'd obviously wanted to go off on his own. And Buck's lips tightened downward as he tossed the abandoned stern line to the fisherman on the dock. Only Mrs. H was getting exactly what she wanted—a chance to buy a new toy for her son.

BAROMETER *An instrument that measures atmospheric pressure, used at sea to forecast the weather. Also called "the glass."*

3

BY THE TIME MRS. HAVERFORD and her gagging cloud of perfume managed to climb off Surprise, Greg had already charged up the dock and pushed through a line of people. The crowd was waiting to get inside that brick building, all grownups—except for two girls with neat red-brown hair.

A turquoise sign read "National Oceanic and Atmospheric Administration," matching the bow of the white ship out front. Why would so many people want to get inside a science building?

"Have you been here before, Buck?"

"Many times. And I can tell you there's no new iPods in this town—nothing here but science labs and ferry docks and restaurants."

Oliver pointed to the line of people. "What's everyone waiting for?"

"That's the aquarium. Maybe we'll check it out when we come back to pick up your mom."

"Mom's coming?" Oliver squeaked.

"Didn't she tell you? I guess she has an old friend at the Yacht Club." Buck pointed out across the harbor to the next pair of jetties—one wood, one concrete. Overlooking the docks were a compact clubhouse with weathered shingles and a white flagpole.

"She's planning to have lunch with her friend and then sail to Vineyard Haven with us. A course, that's assuming Mrs. H still thinks this cruise is a good idea in a couple days." Buck pressed the skinny bridge of his nose between thumb and forefinger. "Hopefully Greg's attitude has improved by then."

Buck had a right to be tired. They'd cast off early this morning and he'd steered the whole way, trying to get to know Surprise while the owner watched his every move. He probably wished they were already anchored inside Hadley's so he could down his tot of rum, or whatever modern schooner captains drank.

"Could you find a faucet?" Buck asked.

Scrambling over the lifelines onto the dock, Oliver felt the steadiness sway underneath him after a whole day rocking at sea. He walked along a raised edge of thick planking, lining up the heel of one foot with the big toe of the other. Before he'd passed two pilings, he saw a rusty water tap.

Buck had dragged a stiff coil of green garden hose out of Surprise's lazarette. He passed one end up to Oliver.

"Screw this on, then wait for my signal. I've gotta find the key to open the deck fitting."

"Shouldn't you check down below first, to see why the tank leaked?"

"Jeepers!" Buck smacked the side of his head. "I'm not thinking straight. Come back aboard and we'll look together, in case I miss–"

"Ahoy Surprise!" A pencil-thin man in baggy khaki leaned against a piling. "Cap'n Eli aboard?"

Buck shook his head. "Gone to sail the great schooner in the sky, I'm afraid."

The man scratched under his white beard. "Damn, he was only a few years older 'n me. Ran a few cargoes with him, before I took to fishing. Years ago now." Thumbs latching into belt loops, his eyes followed the masts aloft. "He'd be right proud to see his old girl all spiffed up again. Last time I saw Surprise, she was leaking like an old potato sack. Who did the work?"

"Place down in Rhode Island—Dutch Harbor Boat Yard."

"Ayuh—I hear they do a good job spiffin' up old boats."

"That they do." Buck dropped a hand onto Oliver's shoulder. "This boy's mother runs the place."

"Really! I thought it was some friend of Eli's, a man named Nichols. Or Nicholas–"

"Oliver Nichols—my grandfather," Oliver blurted out. "He died, last summer. He was Cap'n Eli's best friend." And mine too, he wanted to add.

"I'm sorry to hear that."

Maybe this khaki guy knew Eli when he worked for Grampa as a boatyard mechanic. Like in 1938, before he'd owned Surprise, when he was already talking about tossing her stubborn engine overboard...

Even if it had been just a dream, getting to know Cap'n Eli and Grampa as young men had been awesome.

The man's gaze returned to Buck. "Going to Hadley's to ride out the blow tonight?"

"Yeah—we just came in to fill the water tanks."

"Make sure to let the water run a bit first. Otherwise it'll taste like old seaboots."

Buck led the way down the companionway ladder. On the bottom step he paused to tap the barometer.

"Still dropping...hmm." Next he tapped the ship's clock, even though the hands were stopped at two-twenty-five.

"I'll get that thing running again," Buck promised. "Probably just needs oiling."

The barometer and clock were mounted on the aft bulkhead, just above a built-in bench and table where Eli had kept his charts. This cozy cabin had been his bedroom, kitchen, den, and bathroom. That was the only thing Mrs. H had changed—Eli's ancient cedar bucket and short partition had been replaced by a toilet that disappeared completely behind a full-height door. "A city girl has her limits," she'd said.

She would sleep in the aft bunk on the starboard side, just above the large floral bag gaping open on the settee. The forward bunk dripped with white electrical cords—Greg had marked his territory.

On the port side of the cabin, Oliver's duffle bag was still zipped neatly shut. And only a small blue pillow lay in the captain's bunk, right next to the companionway.

Oliver knelt down beside Buck, inhaling a mix of mint, sunscreen, and sweat. Now that the bilge was dry, it was easy to see a hose dangling loose from the forward end of the water tank.

"That explains the leak." Buck glanced over at Oliver. "You know anything about this?"

"No. But it seems kinda weird—especially with the bilge pump turned off."

"Like someone wanted this trip to be over before it began. And now he's gotten exactly what he was after—a trip ashore." Buck pinched the bridge of his nose again, so hard it stayed white after he let go. "Crazy-ass idea, taking kids that hate sailing out on an old schooner."

"I like sailing."

"Yeah, I know. Otherwise I'd dump this whole mess right back in her highness' shiny lap and hop the next bus back to Newport."

Reaching for the multi-tool he wore on his belt, Buck flicked it open and pulled out a flathead screwdriver. "At least he didn't do any real damage—I'll just reattach the hose. Mind setting us up for a refill?"

Back on deck, the building breeze whistled in the rigging overhead. Clouds slid by, slivers of white against a graying sky.

"Gonna blow tonight." The khaki man still leaned against the same piling.

"Yes sir." Oliver pulled himself up onto the dock.

A knob-knuckled finger pointed at the two red socks embroidered on Oliver's blue T-shirt. "Baseball fan?"

"Yes, sir!"

"Where ya from?"

"Jamestown, Rhode Island."

"Ayuh. I spent some time down in Newport, back when me and Eli was in our prime. We sure had some fun."

"Did you know my grandfather too?"

Mr. Khaki shrugged. "I mighta met him once or twice. I do remember when his wife died, though. Eli disappeared for a couple weeks, and somebody spread a nasty rumor that Surprise had sunk. Turned out he'd hopped back to Rhode Island to help your Grampa."

Grandma Nellie. She'd died just a few months after Mom was born.

Oliver wanted to ask more questions, but Buck was waiting. Pulling the hose tail down the dock, he screwed the end onto the faucet before remembering the old geezer's words—let the water run. Reddish brown water pulsed into the harbor.

"That's right, son." The khaki guy had followed him. "Let 'er run till she's clear—there ya go."

Ten minutes later, the tank had been topped off again with (according to Mr. Khaki) the best tasting water in all of New England. Coiling up the stiff new hose, Oliver remembered the drudgery of yard work at home. Taking care of Surprise didn't feel anything like work.

"Where are those two?" Buck looked up at the sky. "Maybe we should just leave 'em here." On deck they were in the lee of the aquarium, but overhead the stiffening breeze pressed against masts and rigging, heeling Surprise toward the dock.

He pulled two mints out of his pocket. "Want one?"

"No thanks."

"Can't blame you—they taste lousy." The mint clicked against his teeth. "But I figure sugar will kill me slower than nicotine. I gotta do something to keep off the smokes this–"

"Better get away from the dock before the wind pipes up anymore," Mr. Khaki called. "I can help with your lines."

Buck crossed to the starboard rail. "Thanks, but I gotta wait for the owner."

"In my day, if the owners wanted to come along we just gave 'em a whiff of the cargo. That put 'em off the idea quick enough."

"They are the cargo," Buck replied.

"Ayuh. And don't they smell?" The old guy's chuckle turned into a lung-busting cough.

The snap of luffing canvas drew Oliver's gaze out to the harbor. Off the Yacht Club, sails on several small boats crept up stubby masts. An evening race, probably. One blue boat sailed out of the cove on the other side of the town dock, steered by a woman in a yellow rain jacket with a thick bundle of brown hair. Up forward sat a dark-haired boy a little younger than Oliver. He was wearing a red lifejacket, and when he saw Oliver watching he stuck out his tongue.

Oliver had been itching to race—Mom said he could start next year—but even that jeering tongue didn't make him jealous. The deck of Surprise was where he belonged.

Still, he couldn't help answering.

"Oliver, really! Don't stick your tongue out like that—it's quite rude." Mrs. H reached her two plastic shopping bags across the gap between boat and dock. "Take these, please."

Greg sauntered up behind her, staring at what must be an even smaller screen hidden in his left palm.

"A quart of the best clam chowder on Cape Cod, according to the locals," she said. "We'll have it for dinner tonight—"

"Mother! You know I prefer Manhattan-style."

"That's why I went to two different places. I got a quart of each." She smiled back at Greg. "And we also met a lovely girl in the coffee shop who sold us her music player. For more than it was worth, of course."

Removing her clacky sandals, Mrs. H clambered back onto Surprise. "We'll save your mother's stew for tomorrow," she told Oliver.

"Actually my dad made—"

"Could we get going?" Buck interrupted.

Greg climbed aboard and headed below. Oliver handed the bags down the ladder to Mrs. Haverford. By the time she returned on deck, Buck had already started the engine and Mr. Khaki had cast off the stern line.

With the wind pinning them onto the upwind side of the dock, Surprise would scrape her fresh paint along the pilings if they tried to motor straight out. So instead Buck inched the schooner forward, instructing Mrs H and Oliver to hold fenders between the topsides and each tarred piling. Once Surprise reached the end of the dock the bow blew downwind, pivoting on Oliver's fender. Gunning the engine in reverse, Buck quickly backed away into the breeze.

"Thanks much!" Buck waved goodbye to Mr. Khaki, adding under his breath, "And hopefully that's the last trip ashore for a few days."

WOODS HOLE PASSAGE *A channel connecting Buzzards Bay to Vineyard Sound. The current runs so fast because the tidal range is greater in the Bay than the Sound.*

T HE DIESEL EASILY POWERED SURPRISE into the puffy wind and back across the harbor again. They passed by the small town, where a drawbridge had opened for a white sailboat. The chart showed a round cove inside called Eel Pond, deep enough even for Surprise if she could fit through the bridge. That must be a great hurricane hole too.

They rounded Grassy Island, giving Buck's rock a wide berth, and entered the Hole. The current still ran west so it pushed them along, but the water had slowed so much the fat red and green buoys stood almost vertical.

Funny there wasn't more in Cap'n Eli's log about this rocky passage. Sailing through here must've been a challenge, no matter which way the current flowed.

The rocky gargoyles guarding the entrance to Hadley's sported a furry beard of seaweed halfway up their sides. Oliver could have touched their heads with a long pole as the schooner passed between them. Instead he watched the depth sounder hold steady at twelve feet, which just didn't seem possible in such a narrow strip of water. Then they entered the harbor, and he forgot to wonder about anything except the magic of this almost landlocked cove.

The water showed only a ruffle of wind. Trees grew all around, a tall canopy of green spiked with stems of dark pointed fir. On the far shore, a lone deer ambled across the tiny beach.

The main harbor opened up to starboard. They motored past a small floating dock where a few skiffs bumped alongside.

"Bull Island." Buck nodded to the hump of land now hiding the outer harbor. "You can check it out tomorrow. Give you a chance to get off Surprise and run around a bit."

"I don't want to get off her," Oliver replied.

"You sure got a thing for this boat."

Oliver grinned. "Yup, I do."

Up ahead, beyond all the shiny yachts swinging on white mooring balls, a skinny channel disappeared under a wooden bridge.

"Where does that go?"

"Back out to Buzzards Bay."

"And one family really owns this whole island?"

"Look at the chart—it's a whole bunch of islands clustered together. And a bunch of families, now—descendants of the original owner. Fortunately they haven't sold out to a developer yet."

Buck pulled the black knob of throttle back to vertical, slowing Surprise to a crawl. The harbor opened up again, this time to port—where another cluster of boats waited for the next adventure.

On shore, a red boathouse stood guard over a long dock and a string of matching sailboats.

"You can really step back in time out here." Buck pointed to the stubby varnished masts lining the dock. "Most of those day

boats are older than Surprise. They just got more lovin' over the years—and never carried anything heavier than a few people."

Buck wound the wheel two spokes to port. "Thanks to our Woods Hole detour, we're too late to get a guest mooring. We'll have to anchor."

Cap'n Eli's last log entry about Hadley's had predicted just that:

> COAST GUARD ADDED VISITOR MOORINGS TO INNER HARBOR. NOW ALL THE SISSY YACHTS WILL STAY FOR A WEEK AND IT'LL BE TOO CROWDED TO RIDE OUT A BLOW.

Surprise arced her slow pirouette around a dark blue sailboat with paint peeling off the coamings and a cover flapping halfheartedly against the sail it was supposed to protect. The gold leaf on the transom was still readable—*Mariah*.

"That's what Surprise looked like, last summer," Oliver told Buck.

"Really? Hard to believe, now she's all bright and shiny."

Almost as shiny as the "day boats" they were sliding past again. Crisp red sails stretched along varnished booms, all ready for an afternoon cruise.

They rounded the rocky corner across from Bull Island just as Mrs. Haverford's head appeared in the main companionway.

"I'm making some cheese and crackers. How long until we're finally stopped?"

"Not long now, ma'am."

Buck turned to Oliver.

"Mind getting the new anchor ready?"

The fresh planking was still warm underfoot. Up in the very bow, a stainless box with a sideways winch and a thick-toothed gear had been bolted into the foredeck. This would be the first test of the new electric windlass.

Careful of his fingers, Oliver flipped up the flat shiny stop and ran his eye along the heavy chain. It appeared out of a hole in the deck, locked in tight for a right angle turn around the gear, and ran forward to shackle into the anchor. Perfect. Now all he had to do was push his big toe against the down switch when Buck was ready.

Surprise turned into the wind, the propeller's rumble fading as Buck shifted into neutral. A sharper vibration announced reverse. Oliver watched the trees off the port side, waiting for the boat to stop moving forward.

When she hovered, ready to fall back on her heels, Buck nodded. "Let go!"

Pressing the foot button, Oliver watched the chain clunk over the side, loud enough to spook the deer in the woods. Once the freefall stopped, the links inched out one at a time. The anchor had found bottom.

"Not very deep," Oliver said when Buck came forward.

"Fourteen feet, and the stickiest anchor-holding mud around. That's why it's such a great hurricane hole." He eyed the scudding clouds overhead. "It can blow stink from any direction and the only thing to worry about is other boats dragging down on you."

"Nothing upwind of us here except trees—and that deer."

"That'll change tonight." Buck nodded past the rocky point to starboard, back toward Mariah, the sailboat with the sun-rotted sailcover.

"How do you know the wind'll shift that way?"

"Hold out your right arm—no, off to the side of your body—and slightly abaft the beam." Oliver pointed slightly behind him. "Now face into the wind—there! Your arm's pointing toward where the nearest low is. Which direction is that?"

"Northwest."

"Exactly. So when that low goes by tonight–" he pulled Oliver's arm back, forcing his body to spin to the right— "the wind will veer, or push into the west. Understand?"

"Wow, that's cool!"

"Very cool. And that and a dollar fifty might still buy you a cup a coffee somewhere."

Eyeing the angle of chain as it met the water, Buck clanked out another ten feet. "Sixty feet should be plenty. We don't want to christen this new anchor by dragging onto someone else." Opening a small locker in the deck, he pulled out a fat metal hook spliced into a short white line.

"What's that?"

"Snubber—keeps that fancy new bronze chock from getting chewed up by the chain running over it." Locking the hook into a link, Buck tied the line off to the cleat and tapped the foot button, sending the hook overboard. Once the strain was on the line instead of the chain, he nodded.

"Now we're set for the night." He lowered his voice almost to a whisper. "Let's just keep the whole water tank thing between us for now, okay?"

COCKPIT *An enclosed area from which a boat is steered, which serves as a gathering place while in harbor.*

5

ONE HOUR LATER, OLIVER LEANED back against the cockpit seat to stretch his very full belly. After cheese and crackers, he'd had a bowl of each kind of chowder. He definitely liked the creamy kind better—the Manhattan-style tasted like spaghetti sauce had fallen into the pot by mistake.

Greg'd set down his new MP3 player just long enough to wolf down two bowls of the red stuff. Oliver couldn't decide which would be less rude—should Greg lose his earphones so they all could hear, or just go below?

It wasn't like he would miss any real conversation. After a ten minute monologue on how much Greg would learn this week (to row, to steer, to hoist a sail), Mrs. H. asked Buck where they would sail tomorrow. And her voice underlined the word "sail."

"Depends on how quick this storm blows through," Buck said, popping an after-dinner mint. "We'll figure it out in the morning."

"That sunset doesn't look like a storm." Mrs. H pointed west, under the bottom edge of the cockpit awning that whipped and crackled in the salty breeze. "Isn't it beautiful?"

Behind a pointy-roofed house on the far hill, the setting sun poured through a fresh slit in the clouds. Oliver shivered, though the air on his bare arms and legs was still warm. Red sky at night, sailor's delight—somehow, that slice of bloody sky didn't look at all delightful.

"Before it gets too dark," Mrs. Haverford announced, "I will read from Father's log. Do you know, he was in this very harbor, fifty-five years ago today? Let me just get–"

She climbed below. From the aft corner of the cockpit, Buck sighed. "Just what we need, a history lesson from Cap'n Eli."

Oliver grinned. "Don't worry. He wasn't exactly long-winded."

The familiar blue cover came up the companionway, death-gripped between Mrs. Haverford's pink nails. Perched once again on the port cockpit seat, she licked her right index finger and paged ahead to a yellow sticky note.

"Ah, here we are!" She looked around the cockpit expectantly. "I'll start a few days earlier, on August 26, 1954:

FAIRHAVEN TO CUTTYHUNK WITH FIREWOOD. PICKED UP ANOTHER SHIP'S BOY. CAN'T BE BOTHERED TO LEARN THEIR NAMES ANYMORE, SO I'M JUST CALLING HIM 'BOY.' RESPLICED A CHAFE SPOT IN THE MAINSHEET AND END FOR ENDED IT ONCE IN HARBOR..."

Mrs. Haverford's squeal hurt his ears. But it was awesome to hear Cap'n Eli's familiar words again, onboard Surprise in this harbor he'd heard so much about.

"*...OFF-LOADED AT CUTTYHUNK COAST GUARD STATION. QUIET NIGHT. TO VINEYARD HAVEN TOMORROW. COAST GUARD CAPTAIN REPORTS LOW PRESSURE OFF BAHAMAS.*"

Mrs. H glanced up at her son. Greg's eyes remained on his video.

"AUGUST *28*. WIND SOUTHWEST FORCE *3*, STEADY GLASS. NEW BOY COULDN'T TELL PORT FROM STARBOARD SO LEFT HIM ON THE DOCK. NO CARGO, SO NO HELP NEEDED..."

"Cap'n Buck, can you tell us what 'force three' means?"

"It's part of the Beaufort scale," Buck replied. "Zero's a flat calm, twelve's a hurricane. Force three would be a nice easy breeze like we had this morning."

"And what's a steady glass?"

"A glass is the barometer—probably the same one that's mounted on the bulkhead below. It measures pressure." His mint clicked against his teeth. "Steady or rising means good weather."

"That's so helpful! Thank you." She ran her finger down the page.

"AUGUST *30*. WIND SOUTHWEST FORCE *4*, GLASS FALLING—"

She glanced over at Buck. "So that would mean bad weather?"

"On its way, yup."

"This is so wonderful!" Her smile leaped to Greg. "We're learning from your grandfather, even after he's gone."

She flipped to a new page.

"LOAD OF CLAMS FOR NEW BEDFORD. BORROWED CAP'N ROB'S BOY AND MADE IT TO HADLEY HARBOR BEFORE THE CURRENT TURNED AGAINST US. BOY STOOD ANCHOR WATCH LAST NIGHT SO FINALLY GOT SOME SLEEP. CAP'N ROB SAID LOW'S OFF HATTERAS, TRACK SAME AS '*38*."

Again her white teeth gleamed up at Greg.
"Isn't this so exciting?"

If she really wanted to interest him in his grandfather's life, she'd have to make a movie out of it.

"'August 31,'" she continued.

> "WIND SOUTHWEST FORCE 5, GLASS FALLING HARD. A FEW YACHTS IN HERE TOO, PLUS USUAL FAMILY BOATS. SET SECOND ANCHOR TO NORTHWEST, LATE."

The book slammed shut so hard even Greg looked up.

"I'm going to keep you all in suspense—we'll read the next entry tomorrow. Now I'll get at those dishes." And Mrs. H climbed back down the companionway, carrying the book away.

Oliver's fingers itched for the log. Mrs. H had stopped just before the best entry about Hurricane Carol:

> HADLEY SAVED US AGAIN. STARLIGHT ASHORE. CLAMS WERE STARTING TO STINK SO SAILED ON THE MORNING TIDE. WIND NW FORCE FIVE TO SIX, ON THE NOSE TO NEW BEDFORD. TIED UP JUST BEFORE SUNSET, EIGHT HOURS TO GO FOURTEEN MILES. BUT FIRST IN SO PRICE BEST EVER.

Reading the log at home, he'd wondered how choosing the right harbor could make such a difference. Now that he'd seen the green hills wrapping around this cozy basin, he understood.

Buck stretched his arms overhead. "Time to make colors. Greg, want to do the honors?"

Greg flicked thick bangs out of his eyes. "What's that mean?"

"Lowering the flags. It's traditional at sunset."

"So why don't you just say that? I don't understand why boats need their own language."

"Oliver?" It came out as a sigh.

"Just the ensign?"

"Please. We'll leave the Surprise flag up tonight."

Buck'd been handed the crisp private signal that morning—a

large red face with an "O" for a mouth, plastered on a bright yellow background—with orders to fly it from the mainmast. He was probably trying to wear it out as fast as possible.

Back aft, the stars and stripes flapped against the transom. Oliver lifted the varnished staff out of its bronze socket and rolled up the flag.

"Where should I—oh yeah! In the lazarette."

"That crazy word again," Greg muttered.

Buck stood up. "I'm gonna go check the anchor and get some sleep. If it blows as hard as they say after midnight, this might be my only chance."

"Want me to stand anchor watch?" Oliver asked.

Buck reached out to tousle his hair. "No need for that. You might want to turn in too."

"I can sleep when I get home—this is way too cool."

"What's so cool about it?" Greg asked, almost as if he really wanted to know.

When Oliver didn't answer, Greg shuffled off below.

Oliver leaned his head back over the cockpit coaming, trying to identify the stars playing hide and seek behind the racing clouds. Maybe he could find a way to be the ship's boy on Surprise next summer. He'd be fourteen then, and Mom would help him get his license. Mrs. H said she wanted to take Surprise to Maine or even Nova Scotia, and Buck couldn't do that on his own. Now that would be really cool—especially if Greg stayed ashore.

If only Eli was here, to explain everything. The log was great, but he'd just written down the unusual stuff. If Oliver ever kept a journal he wouldn't bother to say what his dad made him for lunch every day.

And Cap'n Eli definitely wouldn't be so patient with his human cargo. Even if they were family...

Oliver's eyelids drooped. He'd just nap for a few minutes, here on the cockpit seat.

6

~

THE FEVER CAME ON EVEN faster than last winter's flu. Head burning against his hands, Oliver thrashed around to escape the demons invading his body. He finally landed in the bottom of the cockpit, trying not to moan. Instead he clutched his forehead in one hand and a belly of fire in the other.

After some unmeasurable agony of time, the fever and bellyache lessened. A steady thunk of halyards against the mast told him the wind had come up just as Buck predicted—or maybe harder. Surprise was pulling on her anchor chain like a jumpy dog.

"Ohhh."

The moan from the companionway ladder was even deeper than the wind's howl.

"What's happening to me?" The long-haired silhouette had to be Greg. "I can barely breathe, and I'm burning up—I need some air." He tumbled into the bottom of the cockpit.

"Ow—get off my leg!" Oliver shoved him forward. "I feel like crap too. Must've been the red chowder." Another snap at the chain pulled Surprise up taut.

"Make this boat stop moving," Greg moaned.

Oliver crawled back up onto the cockpit seat, head spinning. Surprise lurched and bucked, and something up forward squealed, metal against metal.

"I'm gonna check the anchor." He grabbed onto the lifelines to stumble forward.

The squeal was easy to find—it was the anchor chain, rasping and sawing at the chock. The snubber and the hook dangled loose—the line must've stretched so much it dropped off the chain. He managed to hook it into a link again without letting his fingers get between the chain and the chock, where they'd probably be sliced right off. Then he released the stop on the windlass to ease out a few more links—but where was the foot switch? The deck on the starboard side of the windlass was bare.

He'd better wake Buck. Hard to believe he hadn't woken up on his own with all the straining and screeching—but maybe he'd eaten the red chowder too.

Oliver crawled aft, trying not to wince when the chain pulled up short. He headed straight for the companionway.

"What're you doing?" Greg asked.

"I've gotta wake Buck. The snubber came undone."

"He's not down there—nobody is! And it smells like seaweed. We're all alone on this crap boat–"

"Don't you talk about Surprise that way!" Oliver raised a finger to Greg's face. "She's better than two of you."

His toes found the first step of the companionway ladder by feel.

Buck's bunk was empty—even the blue pillow was gone.

He almost fell off the ladder when Surprise jerked hard to port. She'd pull the anchor right out of the bottom unless he could figure out how to get that snubber to stay on the chain.

After crawling up to the bow again, he felt around the entire triangle of foredeck for the windlass foot button. The wood was smooth either side of the boxy winch. Smooth, and a bit worn—time for oil already? Jeez, the boat just came out of the shop a few weeks ago.

Behind him a length of pipe poked up. It looked just like the old windlass handle, and it fit right into the slot on top. Pumping it back and forth, he got the chain to ease until the groaning of metal on metal was replaced by the creak of thick line under a huge load. Still scary, but way better.

This was some blow! And now he felt rain needling against his neck. Stumbling back to the cockpit, he collapsed on the starboard seat. A wave of dizzy heat rushed to his head—the fever was returning.

Another groan from the cockpit floor—Greg hadn't moved. Oliver kicked bare toes against the curled-up back.

"Get up. We've gotta figure out where everyone is."

"Isn't it obvious, Sherlock? They've left us."

"Buck would never leave this schooner. And neither would your mom."

"First thing I'd do, if I had a choice."

Something didn't feel right about the whole situation, and it wasn't just two missing people or trying to talk sense into Greg.

"Look, maybe we should just go back to sleep. We might be dreaming."

"Both of us?" Greg snorted. "Dumbest thing I ever heard."

Oliver stood up, sending his head spinning again. "I'm going below. Anyway it's raining–"

No awning! Had it blown away? He couldn't think about that right now—he had to lie down.

Crawling down the ladder again into the cabin, Oliver inhaled carefully. Seaweed for sure, and something else that reminded him of cleaning winches at the boatyard—kerosene. And clams—ugh! His gut shifted. Hadn't Mrs. Haverford washed the dinner dishes? He wouldn't eat anymore of that red chowder, no matter what the Woods Hole locals said.

Must put his head down—now. Crawling into his bunk, he landed on a bag of what felt like straw. And when he stretched out his feet, his duffle bag wasn't at the forward end. If Mrs. H unpacked it he'd be—

"Oh, my stomach." Greg lurched down the ladder and onto the starboard settee, hands tight against his belly.

Lying down, Oliver's head stopped spinning. Opening his eyes again, he peered across the dark cabin.

Greg sprawled on the opposite settee, apparently too weak to crawl up into his bunk. Further aft, the bunk was empty— not even a flowered bag. Where were Buck and Mrs. H? There weren't many places to hide on Surprise, and he couldn't picture them rowing ashore in the stormy dark.

The ship's clock chimed a friendly three bells—Buck must've fixed it, as promised.

And in the middle of the cabin, the stove loomed—black and large. Just like the one he'd seen aboard Surprise when he'd stumbled back to 1938…

Not again!

Could he be hallucinating, from the fever?

He closed his eyes, willing his heart to stop pounding.

In the morning, he promised himself, it would all make sense.

SHIP'S CLOCK *A full cycle of the ship's clock lasts four hours, the traditional time for a sailor to stand watch. One bell is added every half-hour, up to eight bells.*

7

WHEN HE WOKE AGAIN, a gray gloom filled the skylight and the wind in the rigging whistled louder than he'd ever heard before.

No more stomach cramps or fever, which was a relief. But his left shoulder felt damp—jeez, the deck was leaking!

Oliver slid inboard as far as he could, away from the drip running down the outboard side of his bunk. Mom would be totally pissed. She'd made sure the workers covered every inch of the old deck in plywood and epoxy, telling everyone there was nothing worse than sleeping in a wet bunk.

The ship's clock chimed five bells—six-thirty. A cheery greeting on this gray day.

Surprise lurched to starboard, tugging on her chain. So the anchor was still holding, even though it was blowing really, really hard.

Swinging his legs out of his bunk, Oliver braced for the dizziness to return. But his stomach rumbled only with emptiness.

Greg sprawled dead to the world on the starboard settee, one arm thrown over his head and his mouth hanging open. At least he wasn't whining in his sleep.

Opening the companionway hatch let in a wall of rain, so Oliver slid it closed and glanced out the portlight instead. Spray blew off the wave tops, as high as Surprise's cabin—in Hadley's, the best harbor on the east coast!

No Buck, no Mrs. H. Only Surprise, and useless Greg Haverford, here in the middle of what looked like a hurricane.

So what exactly was he supposed to do now?

"Coffee makes any day seem brighter, Oliver. Just the smell is a whiff of stomach-warming hope." The voice was as clear as if Grampa were standing right next to him.

When Grampa turned the boatyard over to Mom, he'd moved into their spare room. Every day after school he'd helped Oliver whip up a snack in the "galley," which is what he called the kitchen even at home. Most days that snack included coffee. Grampa drank his black, but he added a dollop of milk and a huge spoonful of sugar to Oliver's mug.

Okay then, he'd make coffee.

A dented kettle waited on the stove. Oliver pulled up on the round black handle next to the sink, but nothing happened. Huh, it was hanging over the edge just like a faucet. Moving the kettle away, he pushed the handle back down—and water gushed out! Way cool.

He had so much fun pumping water into the kettle he could barely lift it back onto the burner. Now, how to light it? The black valves along the front all looked the same...

This could really get overwhelming if he didn't focus.

Matches? On the shelf right above him, in a jar. He pulled one out, wondering what to strike it on, until he set the jar down and the bottom scratched at the counter. Flame to burner, valve open...

Nothing. But some sort of liquid pooled around the other

burner, so he must've turned the wrong valve. He moved the match over and–

WHOOSH! A sheet of fire shot up, singeing his bangs. He quickly turned it down, and the flame sputtered out. Shoot— he'd just have to try again.

This time he slid the kettle over the burner when the flame leaped up again. Now while the water boiled he could try to figure out what was going–

"Hey, it's raining on me!" Rolling off the settee, Greg landed on the cabin sole. "What's with this boat anyway?"

"Deck's leaking." A drip hissed onto the stove, so Oliver lined up a rusty coffee can to catch the next one. Rain spattered against the skylight.

"What a piece of..."

Greg's voice trailed off when Oliver turned to glare at him.

Sliding open the nearest locker, Oliver found a dented canister full of coffee and an enamel pot. When the kettle whistled he poured boiling water over the grounds, breathing in the steamy roasted scent of those afternoons with Grampa. They'd sit at the kitchen table and talk about Oliver's day at school, or about whatever Grampa was whittling. A lump rose in his throat so big it was hard to swallow.

"Wow, that doesn't smell half bad." Greg hadn't moved from the cabin sole. "My mom won't make coffee at home—says it's too hard."

"My grampa would say it smells like hope."

"How long do you brew it?"

Oliver had no idea, and he remembered Grampa pressing down the grounds. This pot wasn't that fancy.

"It's ready," he said. "Want some?"

"I guess—sure smells good."

Oliver filled the two white mugs he'd found hanging above the sink. Looked about right—brown and hot, anyway. Sugar and milk? Mrs. H had told him to stay out of the icebox, but this was an emergency.

He'd check the lockers first, since sugar was way more important. Not the coffee locker—how about the small one to the left of the stove? Bingo! Salt, pepper, hot sauce, and sugar lined the top shelf. And a small can with two round holes in the top—condensed milk. He pulled that out too.

The lower shelf held a nautical jumble—a roll of marlin, a knife with a marlinspike just like the one Eli always carried, one rusty whistle, and a greenish bronze tube flared like a trumpet.

"What's that?" Greg pointed at the tube.

"Foghorn." Oliver blew a goose-like honk. "I won't go full volume—wake the dead."

"You don't suppose we're dead, do you?"

More likely, they hadn't been born yet.

Crawling to his knees, Greg pointed a finger at Oliver. "You killed my mother, didn't you? And Buck too! You poisoned us with that chowder, and then tossed their bodies to the sharks—"

Oliver snorted. "There aren't any sharks in here. And if I'd poisoned the chowder, I wouldn't have eaten any. Then I wouldn't have gotten sick, and I wouldn't be here with you." He raised the coffee pot. "I'm gonna make yours the same way I make my own, okay?"

Scowling, Greg collapsed back onto his butt and wrapped pale arms around the black knees of his jeans. Oliver turned back to the counter, feeling the dark eyes drilling between his shoulder blades.

Stirring in a dollop of condensed milk and a large spoonful of sugar, he passed a mug to Greg. Then he sat down on the port settee with his own mug warm between his palms.

"I think—I'm pretty sure we've gone back in time."

"What? How did–"

"Let me finish, will you?" Oliver glared across the cabin, and Greg's mouth closed again.

"Last summer, I hit my head and fell back into 1938. I got to know my grandfather, which was really cool. Eli—your grandfather—was just a teenager. There's something about this schooner…"

He glanced around the familiar cabin. If he was dreaming, the detail was incredible. He could feel the hard settee under his butt, could even sense the damp soaking through his shorts from the thin canvas pad. Mom's workers had done a great job recreating this atmosphere—except for the leaks, the oiled wood, and the finicky stove.

"I think time piles up like layers," Oliver said at last. "You can end up in another decade if you find a thin spot. Surprise seems to be one of those—she hasn't changed much in seventy years."

"So…what day is it?"

"I'm not even sure what year it is! But it sure seems like we're in the middle of a hurricane. It can't be 1938 since she was hauled out for that one. Could be 1944, or '54. And there was a crazy storm in 1961, Esther. Did a big loop off the—"

"How come you know so much about hurricanes?"

Oliver shrugged the still-wet shoulder of his T-shirt. "After almost living through a really big one, I wanted to learn about the rest." He stood up, peeked out through the portlight, and sat back down again, blowing across his mocha-colored coffee. "Hadley's probably hasn't changed much in the past hundred years. I don't know how you figure out what year it is when there's no one around."

"Does it matter?" Greg placed the mug on his knees and rested his forehead against the rim. "We're stuck here until someone comes to rescue us."

"Nobody's coming—we'll have to save ourselves. And we won't know how to do that until we figure out what year it is."

"Huh?"

"We have to fit in to find our way home."

"Fitting in sucks."

"Not if it saves your life." Oliver blew again on his coffee, curling steam toward Greg. "What would you do with some kid that showed up at your school and said he was from a different century?"

"Lynch 'em."

"Exactly. So the only way we survive this is to fit in." Oliver stared across at Greg's left ear. "Which means those earrings have to go."

Greg fingered the two silver loops. "You're just gonna give up?"

"Fitting in isn't giving up—it's how we survive, until we get back to our own time."

"And how do we do that?"

"Jeez, haven't you been listening? I don't know yet!"

Greg stretched out one leg to reach into his right pocket. "At least I've got my phone. I can try calling my—hey! I've got no signal!"

This was going to be a very long day.

CABIN SOLE *The collection of floorboards used to cover the deep interior or bilge in the living spaces of a boat.*

8

STANDING UP TO RINSE OUT his empty coffee mug, Oliver heard a thump against the outside of the hull. Had another boat dragged down on Surprise? He eyed the companionway hatch, wondering if he should brave the rain to check—and then the hatch slid back on its own. What the—

"Eli!"

"Cap'n Eli to you, boy. Jaysus it's fierce out there." He stomped down the ladder, slammed the hatch closed over his head, and peeled off a drenched canvas shirt. Next he stripped off his sopping white T-shirt, exposing a tan chest with a mat of blond fuzz. After rubbing at his curls, he draped the two shirts over the companionway ladder. Then he turned back toward the stove.

"Hope that coffee I smell is better than the last brew you—" he stopped, his two bleached eyebrows merging into one bushy line. "Your hair's different. Longer maybe? Or darker."

Oliver forced himself to shrug. "I just slept on it funny. Can I get you some–"

"And who might you be?" Cap'n Eli had spotted Greg.

Greg covered his left ear with a shaking hand. "I–"

"Castaway, sir," Oliver replied quickly. "I, ah—found him clinging to the anchor chain when I checked it last, so I pulled him aboard."

"Not a member of the local family, are ya?"

Greg shook his head.

"Good—most of 'em wouldn't know an honest day's work if it bit 'em in the arse. What's your name? I can't be calling both of you 'boy.'"

"Greg."

"Greg, sir," Eli corrected.

"Huh."

Like a flash of lightning, Cap'n Eli crossed the small cabin and cuffed Greg on the side of the head, drawing out a squeal that sounded like "sir." Oliver grinned, remembering the sting of that meaty hand.

"Awful fancy wristwatch to take swimming, Castaway Greg."

Greg covered the silver bezel with his free hand, staring up at Eli.

Eli turned back to Oliver.

"I got that mother of a second anchor out, no thanks to you asleep in your bunk like we're on a holiday cruise. Even with all their newfangled modern technology the damn weathermen still got it wrong. And I trusted 'em, instead of trusting my own nose. Didn't I tell you last night it was gonna blow? This is worse than anything I've seen since '38."

"A hurricane, sir?"

"Might be. Won't know till they tell us, and by then it'll all be over."

On one of the last visits to see Eli in the hospital, Oliver had asked what year he'd bought Surprise. The old man didn't even recognize his own daughter anymore, but he'd remembered the exact date.

"October 12, 1948," he'd wheezed. "Soon as I got back from the war and made enough money."

So it was after 1948, and judging by Cap'n Eli's muscular shoulders not too much after. 1954 was probably right—that'd make Eli thirty-four. The year his mom was born!

Just behind the companionway ladder—where the new head bulkhead would be on the modern Surprise—Cap'n Eli slit open one of several burlap bags piled up on the cabin sole. They looked like sandbags, stacked to hold back a flood. Jeez, what a stink!

"Might as well eat up some of these quay-hogs, before they go bad." Cap'n Eli pulled out a dull white shell, larger than his hand.

"Ah, captain?" Greg slid something into his pocket—the two earrings. "I don't eat clams. As of last–"

"Then I guess you'll go hungry. What're you doing down there on the sole, anyway? Get up on your two feet and make yourself useful."

Greg shuffled to a standing position, hands dangling down his sides and body swaying with the motion of Surprise. His head just brushed the wood ceiling.

Cap'n Eli's eyes ran up Greg's narrow frame. "Have to earn your keep, you know. You can sweep the floor, for starters. Broom's in that forward locker."

Did Greg even know what a broom looked like? This was gonna be fun to–

"And you, boy—put about ten of those 'hogs in here." Cap'n Eli handed him an enamel bucket. "You can shuck while I get the rest of the chowder ready."

Holding his breath, Oliver pulled out a huge clam. The thing was four times the size of the littlenecks he and Grampa used to dig. It dropped into the bucket with a satisfying clunk.

Whoosh! Fire leaped up from the stove. Arching back to dodge the flame, Cap'n Eli slid a black pan over the burner. Then he pulled an onion out of a net bag hanging next to the sink and began to dice it, with the rigging knife he'd pulled from the sheath on his belt.

Greg swept his way across the cabin, digging into the corners to eke out every little bit of grit. The floor was wet from Cap'n Eli's feet and all the leaks, so most of the dirt stuck to the broom.

Man, those onions smelled good. They'd started to sizzle, on top of what looked like a huge wad of pale butter.

"You'll have to shuck those hogs down here, boy," Cap'n Eli said over his shoulder. "Too dangerous on deck. Work over the bowl so the broom don't end up smelling like clam juice."

"Yes, sir."

"Here's the opener." He tossed Oliver a flat blade. "Remember how I showed you a few days ago? Or maybe that was the last boy. Anyway, cut through the muscle to open the shell. Meat goes in here." He slid a metal bowl across the floor. "Best set on the sole, right there."

Oliver sat down in the middle of the cabin, legs crossed and back against the chart table seat. Sticking the dull blade into the gap between the shells, he tried to pry the two apart. They wouldn't budge.

Dropping the spatula on top of the onions, Cap'n Eli strode aft and grabbed the shell. "That'll never work—clam's stronger than Hercules. You gotta cut the muscle." He sliced all the way to the point, and what he handed back opened easily.

"Cool!"

"Don't make me show you again. And just scoop the whole thing in—don't matter what goes in a chowder."

Oliver slid the knife under the meat, releasing it into the bowl. Tossing the empty shell back in the bucket, he reached for another. After a few tries, Oliver was opening, scooping, and dropping empty shells back in the bucket like he'd been shucking clams his whole life.

"Need that whole bucket done in ten minutes or the onions'll burn."

This stressed-out Cap'n Eli reminded Oliver of his mom when she was worried about making payroll. He was totally different from the two Elis Oliver had already met—the wheezing old man and the teenaged mechanic. Hard to believe this guy would ever smile so wide his skin stretched taut, or wink one of his sparkling blue eyes.

"When are the quahogs supposed to be in port?" Oliver asked, realizing he could talk and shuck at the same time.

Cap'n Eli sighed. "Today. But we won't get out of here before tomorrow at least, and then it'll be an all day slog. Buzzards Bay's a right mother after a storm like this."

"Couldn't you deliver them somewhere else?"

"Like where, the south pole?" Cap'n Eli snorted. "New Bedford's where the buyers are. By the time we get there, everyone will have sold already and the price will be low again."

First in so price best ever.

"Won't everyone else be held up by the weather?"

"Not the trains and the trucks," Cap'n Eli replied. "Nowadays we're racing them too."

Greg had finished sweeping, but he didn't have any idea what to do next. Behind Cap'n Eli's back, Oliver mimed pushing the dirt onto his flattened palm. Greg just stood there, staring—until Cap'n Eli turned around.

"Waiting for flies to land on you?" Cap'n Eli pulled a rusty dustpan out from behind the trash bin and handed it over.

Kneeling down, Greg tried to sweep the dirt into it, but the pan's handle pulled right off—spreading the grit all over Cap'n Eli's bare feet.

"Jesus, Mary and Joseph—ain't you never swept a floor

before?" Stamping his feet, Cap'n Eli swept the pile into the handle-less dustpan and angled it over the trash. Then he handed it back to Greg, opened a nearby drawer, and pulled out a screwdriver.

"What's that?" Greg pointed to the rusty tool.

"A screwdriver! Where you from—Mars?" Cap'n Eli frowned at Greg.

Greg shrugged, a blush flooding across his white cheeks.

A quick turn of the screw and the handle was reattached. Cap'n Eli dropped the dustpan back in its spot and held out the broom. After a slight hesitation, Greg put it back where he'd found it.

When the chowder was ready, Cap'n Eli filled two white bowls and one blue-spotted porcelain bowl. "Eat up good before it goes bad," he said, dropping onto the port settee to slurp steaming broth into his mouth.

Oliver took a small sip. Wow! So much more flavor than last night's chowder—like Mom's, only way more salt and pepper.

Greg pushed his chowder around the speckled bowl, which looked like something for mixing. Cap'n Eli probably only had two regular eating bowls. On Surprise, three was definitely a crowd.

"That's better." With a loud burp, Cap'n Eli set his empty bowl and spoon in the sink. "After the galley's cleaned up we'd best check on the second anchor. I didn't get it set too great so it might not hold, and if it doesn't we'll have to set it again. That'll take all hands in this breeze."

A puff heeled Surprise over sideways. Grabbing the counter, Oliver held his breath until she pulled herself back up into the wind and fell off on to the other tack. Cap'n Eli just shifted his weight from one leg to another.

"Boy, you get the dishes done. Greg can dry for you." Blue eyes pierced him through. "I never noticed before, but you are the spitting image of Otis Nichols, my godson. 'Cept for that mop of hair, a course—his mother'd never allow that, bless her heart."

Eli set one foot on the bottom step of the companionway ladder.

"I'll get another spare anchor line flaked out, just in case. Come up when you're finished in the galley."

And still shirtless, he disappeared up into the storm.

BOWLINE *(pronounced "bo-lin") A knot used to make a secure loop which is easy to untie, even after it's pulled on hard.*

9

"WHAT ARE WE GONNA DO?" Greg squealed as soon as the companionway hatch slammed shut. "The guy's a complete hairball—going up there in a hurricane!"

"He's just trying to keep Surprise safe." Leaning back away from the stove, Oliver lit the correct burner this time and slid the half-full kettle over it.

"But he eats chowder for breakfast!"

"When life gives you clams..."

"What'd you say?"

Oliver sighed. "Can you pass me your bowl?"

Greg handed it over, still full of chowder.

"You gotta eat it," Oliver told him.

"Dump it back in the pot."

"I can't do that!"

"Then eat it yourself—I'm not touching it."

So after a slight hesitation, Oliver took a few bites. Sure was tasty.

Greg crossed ape-like arms over his chest. "I want out," he announced.

"Don't you realize—we're back in 1954! You can't just swim home. We have to wait for a chance to get back to our own time."

"I'm no good at waiting."

"Well, maybe that's why you're here." Oliver finished off the chowder. "And you've really never seen a screwdriver before?"

Greg shook his head.

"Which means you can't have taken that hose off the water tank."

"Huh?" Greg couldn't have faked such a blank look.

Oliver clanked the empty bowl into the sink, on top of Cap'n Eli's. "I'm gonna go help him."

"In all that wind?"

"That's why he needs the help. The stove valve turns off to the right. Hopefully you know how to wash dishes—if not, you'll just have to figure it out."

As soon as Oliver slid back the companionway hatch, the wind tossed all his hair into his eyes. He crawled out into the cockpit, pinning his bangs back with one hand and bracing against Surprise's lurching motion with the other.

The fir trees bent over almost horizontal. White spray blew across the deck. And the waves were bigger than he'd ever seen inside a harbor before.

A skiff just like Sparky, his boat at home, tugged astern of Surprise—empty. Where was Cap'n Eli?

"Boy!" The gasp came from somewhere close to the water. "Toss me a line, quick now."

One meaty hand latched onto the rail of Surprise.

"Cap'n Eli?"

He'd fallen overboard!

Grabbing a tail of the spare anchor line, Oliver tied a quick bowline in one end, dropped the loop over the side, and made the line fast to the stern cleat. Would it work? That's the way he always climbed out of the water after swimming—but he'd never tried it with waves breaking over him.

Cap'n Eli clawed his way hand over hand back along the rail. If he let go, he'd blow downwind so fast there was no way Oliver could rescue him. Oliver watched, heart pounding, as Cap'n Eli grabbed the anchor line, stuck one foot in the loop, grabbed the rail, and heaved himself to a standing position just as the stern bobbed low in the trough of a wave. He could just reach the top lifeline to heave himself aboard.

"Let me help–"

"Out of my way!" Breathing hard, Cap'n Eli stepped over the rail, water streaming off his skin and pants plastered to his legs.

"What happened?"

The wind tore Oliver's words away.

Cap'n Eli waved him forward, shouting, "...below. No way... pray she's dug in..." and then the wind dropped enough so his next words came through loud and clear. "...when the wind swings northwest. Happen right soon, judging by that sun."

Oliver followed Cap'n Eli's finger toward the rays of sunlight beaming through layer after layer of sliding dark clouds. "Is that the eye?"

"Ayuh. Once it goes by, we'll test that second anchor."

"Doesn't the wind usually die when the eye passes overhead?"

"Pretty smart for a ship's boy. Too bad you don't know enough to go below when the weather's foul."

"Not foul now—the sun's coming out." A weird gray-yellow light rolled across the harbor, turning white spray to gold.

"Well, I'm getting below before I catch my death. And I don't want you up here by yourself." Grabbing Oliver's arm, Cap'n Eli pushed him toward the hatch. "Down you be."

LIVED THROUGH A GALE OF WIND LAST NIGHT THAT MIGHT'VE BEEN A HURRICANE. EYE PASSED JUST WEST.

There'd been nothing in the log about going swimming, Oliver was sure. Cap'n Eli must've been too embarrassed to write about that.

Greg had curled up in his bunk, right hand against his ear. At least he'd washed the dishes.

"You okay?" Oliver whispered.

"Stupid question." His narrow hand slipped under the blanket. "When can we go home?"

"I'm working on that. But right now I've got to help Cap'n Eli—he fell overboard."

"Serves him right, going out in such a storm."

"He's trying to take care of Surprise! And she's the only thing taking care of us right now, so give me that blanket."

"No way—I need it." Greg clutched it just below his chin.

"Cap'n Eli needs it more." Whipping the blanket off, Oliver saw a flash of silver. "What's that?"

"Nothing." Greg slid a palm over the shiny rectangle.

"Jeez!" Oliver checked over his shoulder. "Cap'n Eli sees your iPod, he'll think you're from outer space or something."

"My music calms me."

"Better keep it out of sight."

At the bottom of the companionway ladder Cap'n Eli had stripped naked, revealing a sharp line between pasty white legs and brown chest. He'd grabbed his damp T-shirt to dry off. Oliver handed him the blanket.

"Should I make some more coffee, sir?"

"P-please. Smells like hope, you know."

The sudden lump in his throat kept Oliver from answering. If only Grampa were here.

"Once the coffee's made we can heat up the rest of that chowder." Tucking the blanket around himself just below his armpits, Cap'n Eli sat down on the port settee. "Ain't nothing we can do now but eat and sit tight."

"I can't digest chowder," Greg said.

"Well, then don't have any," Cap'n Eli growled. "But it's all you'll get until we make it to New Bedford. And that could be days from now."

"Won't this blow through tonight?" Oliver asked.

"Seems like it. Westerly'll be here soon–" a strong puff pushed the boat over to starboard. "There, she's swinging around now. Storms usually blow the same time from each direction, so it should drop off by dawn."

"And then we can leave?" Greg asked.

"Got a ladyfriend waiting, Castaway Greg?" Cap'n Eli shrugged. "I got a hot date myself, with some clam buyers. But even after the wind dies down enough to sail, we still have to get the anchors up and get out of here. Last fall I rode out a one day storm and spent two days chopping wood to clear the channel."

Greg groaned. "Two days! But I'll–"

Cap'n Eli stood up, crossed the cabin, and whacked Greg on the head, hard.

"Ow!"

"You're lucky to be alive and in a dry bunk."

"It's not dry, there's a leak–"

Another cuff to the side of Greg's head. "Drier than overboard, which is where you'll go back to if you don't stop your whining."

Crossing the cabin again, Cap'n Eli picked his pants up and hung them to drip-dry over the companionway steps. "That coffee ready yet?"

Nobody seemed to want more chowder, so once the coffee was cold and the dishes were clean and dry, there was nothing more to do. Nothing except wait, listen, and cringe at the sharpest tugs on the anchor line.

Cap'n Eli crawled into his bunk and pretended to sleep. Greg rolled himself into a ball on the starboard settee, eyes scrunched shut.

Too restless to lie down, Oliver roamed the cabin. Three books stood on a shelf over the chart table—including the log, though the binding was so smooth and shiny he didn't recognize it at first. It was wedged between a crisp binding stamped in gold with "American Practical Navigator" and a scuffed copy of "Notice to Mariners: Watch Hill, Rhode Island to Monomoy Point, Massachusetts." He pulled that out to flip through it. Dried coffee stained almost every wrinkled page, so Eli must use this book a lot.

But it was totally boring stuff, all latitudes and longitudes and notes about new buoy positions, with not enough names he recognized. Oliver slid it back onto the shelf. That left the other boring book—and the log.

The pencil stuck in the top was so stub-nosed it didn't seem possible for Cap'n Eli to fit more than two or three words on each page. Oliver ran his fingers over the cloth binding, itching to read the familiar words.

But opening it in front of Cap'n Eli felt all wrong, like reading a girl's diary. Pulling away, he stuffed his hands deep into the pockets of his shorts.

Mom had told him there was a reason for everything. So what was he supposed to learn from being here? He already knew Cap'n Eli ran Surprise, had already read the log. This adventure seemed pointless.

Though it sure was fun watching Greg get some discipline for a change.

NAMED STORMS *Since 1953, tropical storms have been named in alphabetical order. Only female names were used until 1979. A list of names is published before hurricane season, which runs from June 1 to November 1. At the end of the season, the names of any severely destructive storms are retired.*

10

I T WAS THE SILENCE THAT woke him.

Oliver had laid awake for hours, wondering how even the great mud of Hadley's could be expected to hold Surprise—she was tugging and tossing and pulling on that second anchor like a frenzied bulldog. And even if the anchor did stay in the mud, the line could easily snap. It was all fuzzy and frayed, not metal-solid like the great links of chain that had kept them in place through the southerly. Then the anchor would be left in the mud and they'd blow downwind onto the rocks, where Surprise would be bashed to pieces and they'd all be tossed into the water–

No. Closing his eyes, he forced himself to inhale a series of deep breaths. Of all the people riding out this storm, he could actually predict the future. After all her bucking and tugging against the anchor line, only to be pulled back head to wind where she would hesitate for a moment before falling off on the other tack—Surprise would make it through the night.

So he'd slept at last, only to wake to this dark silence.

He scrambled out of his bunk and climbed up into the cockpit, clamping arms around his damp shirt to keep from shivering. Off to port, a pale sliver of moon hung over the pointy-roofed house. Dead ahead was the big dipper, each star so clear and sharp it looked like the scoop might actually hold water. The waves had flattened out too, and dark water glinted all around Surprise.

"Barometer's rising again, thank God." Cap'n Eli had come on deck behind him. "And we're still here." Checking their position against the nearest trees, he—at last—winked a lid down over the glimmer of his left eye. "Guess I got that second anchor set just fine, all by myself."

"Guess you did."

"And I'm sure glad not to be sleeping on the beach over there." Eli pointed to Bull Island, now a dark shadow off to starboard. "'Course I probably wouldn't have made it that far, not being able to swim."

"YOU CAN'T SWIM?" Oliver squeaked.

"Sink like a stone every time I try. Usually it keeps me careful, but yesterday—I swear that wind blew me right off my pins." He paused. "Thank you, boy. I owe you my life."

"I don't know about–"

"At the end of my strength I was, when you got that line over. And with a bowline already tied in it! Your dad must've taught you right."

Dad had nothing to do with it, Oliver thought. Mom and Grampa–

"That how you got Greg out of the water too, with a line over the side?"

Oliver shrugged.

"A regular fisher of men you are. Reminds me of a young boy I knew back in '38." Cap'n Eli shook his head. "Poor kid washed away in the hurricane, trying to save Surprise. He had a thing about this schooner, even worse than I did."

Blood rushed to Oliver's face—good thing it was dark. He'd never considered what Grampa and Eli must've thought when he climbed aboard Surprise in 1938 and disappeared. Of course they figured he'd been lost in the storm! That made a lot more sense than what'd actually happened—fast-forwarding back into the twenty-first century.

"What's your name, anyway?"

Oliver hesitated.

"Awh—forget it." Cap'n Eli held up his hand. "I don't want to know. It'll only make it harder when I have to let you go in a few days." Yawning, he stretched his arms overhead. "I'm going back to my bunk, try to get some sleep. You should do the same—be a long hard day tomorrow. Goodnight, boy."

JOHNNYCAKES *A pancake made of cornmeal and hot water or milk, usually lightly sweetened.*

11

SUNBEAMS DANCED THROUGH THE skylight when Oliver woke again. Greg was curled into himself, back to the cabin.

Cap'n Eli stood at the stove.

"Thought I'd make us some johnnycakes," he said. "We'll need our strength for the sailing today."

"Sailing?" Greg rolled over. "Where're we going, Woods Hole?"

"New Bedford—get the clams to market before they're a total loss. And with any luck, we'll pick up a load of something there that needs to get back to Nantucket."

Greg sat up, swinging his feet down onto the settee. "I want to go to Woods Hole."

"I could drop you off on our way by."

"That'd be great–"

"Might even get you pretty close to the beach, so you don't have to swim too far. But I'm not so sure the Penzance Point folks'd think too much of you, all smelly and long-haired and talking back to your elders."

Greg's smile disappeared.

"I've got half a mind to drop you off on Weepecket Island instead," Cap'n Eli continued, sliding the heavy frying pan over the burner. "I'm sure the laughing gulls'd find your guff amusing."

A pulse beating in his right cheek, Greg crossed the cabin in two strides and disappeared up the companionway ladder.

When the johnnycakes were ready, Cap'n Eli divided them up between two plates and a flat bowl and called to Greg to come back below. They polished off the entire stack in silence. Corn-flavored cardboard was a change from chowder, anyway.

Cap'n Eli burped and stood up. "Time to get those anchors out of the mud, boy. Castaway Greg! What's say you do the dishes?"

Greg set the fork down into his empty bowl and swallowed so hard his pointy Adam's apple bobbed twice. Then he nodded.

Before Greg could change his mind, Oliver tossed his plate into the sink and scrambled up the companionway ladder, right behind Cap'n Eli's rubber boots.

"Would ya look at that." Cap'n Eli pointed to starboard, where an enormous sailing yacht lay on her side in the scrub of Bull Island. The long keel stretched out toward Surprise as if asking for help. "That's one of the family boats—Starlight."

STARLIGHT ASHORE.

Now that weird log entry made sense.

"She's been around as long as Surprise and she's worth rebuilding, but these days it's less expensive to cut her up and start over. I hear some guy in Boston's even started building boats in glass fiber! Big mistake if you ask me."

"Why?"

Cap'n Eli shrugged. "Wood floats."

Only a few boats dotted the inner harbor. Farthest into the cove was a dark blue sloop with varnished booms—Mariah! So she made it through this hurricane only to be totally neglected fifty years from now...

The red boathouse overlooked the same lineup of day boats, now half-sunk from all the rain. Just off their dock swung a nice white sloop with a varnished cabin trunk. A dark-haired man standing in the cockpit let go of his camera just long enough for a friendly wave. Cap'n Eli raised one hand in reply and climbed into the skiff.

With long even strokes he rowed them into the stiff breeze all the way to the anchor line, then pulled along it until the line angled almost straight down. Hauling up as hard as he could, he let it bite into the skiff's rail. All that did was heel the skiff over so much that water splashed in. The anchor—dug deep into the mud by Surprise's weight and windage—wasn't budging.

"Might have to put a buoy on it, leave it for now."

The wind blew them back to Surprise. Greg waited in the cockpit, left hand shielding his eyes.

Cap'n Eli climbed aboard. "I'll go get the first anchor put away."

Oliver followed him forward. The windlass happily clunked the chain back on board, each link following its leader down through a hole in the deck, until the huge hook hung suspended above the water. Reaching over the side, Cap'n Eli grabbed the nearest fluke and hooked it over the rail so that most of the anchor stayed outside the hull. So that's why the old rails had a big dent in that one spot!

"That's the easy one," he grunted. "Now take up all the slack you can in that line and hold tight. Castaway Greg! Come up here and help me make sail."

Oliver hauled in the furry wet anchor rode hand over hand while Cap'n Eli and Greg hoisted the mainsail. By the time

Cap'n Eli came forward again, the white rope hung straight down and taut, just as it had from the skiff.

Cap'n Eli glanced to starboard, then to port. "Just enough, I think."

"Enough what?"

"Open water. To sail her out."

"How do you do that?"

"Pull on her sideways." Eli strode aft to the wheel, calling instructions back over his shoulder. "Tie off the bitter end of the anchor line. Then let it run, unless I say different."

Cap'n Eli eased out the enormous mainsail and spun the wheel to port. Slowly, Surprise gathered way on starboard tack, tugging all that wet anchor line back overboard again. As their speed built, the line buzzed out through the chock.

Their course was a beam reach, the fastest angle of sail for Surprise. Only one problem—they were heading straight for the brightly varnished sloop just off the dock. The photographer had vanished, but a wiry man about half the width of Cap'n Eli stood in the cockpit, one hand holding a canvas hat onto his head. The closer they got, the redder the man's face got.

"Ah, Cap'n Eli–"

"Make her fast!"

Oliver snubbed the anchor line around the cleat, screeching them to a halt just before the bowsprit touched the sloop's rigging. Surprise quickly turned into the wind.

Oliver shrugged and smiled at the man, who was so close they could've shaken hands. The mouth-watering aroma of frying bacon drifted up from the small cabin.

"One more try," Cap'n Eli called. "Port tack this time— bring the bow around."

Oliver hauled in the line again, Cap'n Eli trimmed the mainsheet, and slowly Surprise turned away from the sloop and fell onto port tack. Headed toward the entrance they had more room, and Surprise was almost at full speed when the bitter end of the anchor line pulled taut—stopping her short again. A small hesitation as the anchor pulled back on the bow—and then they started crawling forward again, line pulling taut, falling slack, and pulling taut again.

"She's free! Get her off the bottom, boy. Greg, go up there and lend a hand."

With Greg's help, Oliver gathered in hundreds of feet of wet and bristly anchor rode. By the time the actual anchor broke the surface, his right hand had two warm spots. Unclenching his hands, he wasn't surprised to see blisters whitening two of his fingers.

Cap'n Eli came forward, leaving Surprise to creep slowly toward the harbor entrance.

"There she is, the beauty! All that stood between us and the beach." Reaching over the side, he grabbed a fluke and hooked it over the port rail, mirroring the main anchor. A dab of mud flaked with white shell dropped onto the deck. Good holding for sure—sticky as gray-black chewing gum. And stinky, too— the thick dark stench of low tide.

"Boy, you get this mess swabbed down while I get us out of here."

Hmm, swabbed down. That sounded like cleaning, maybe with a mop? Oliver bent over the rail to wipe a few globs off the flukes, and they plopped back into the water like black gumdrops.

"He said you might need this." Greg handed over a mop.

"Thanks. Could you see if there's a bucket?"

"What am I, your servant?"

"I'll be yours, if you clean this muck off the deck."

Greg headed aft again, shoulders rounded inside his T-shirt. He came back quicker than Oliver expected, carrying a metal pail with a short line attached to the handle.

"I'll need some water in that."

"So?"

"So drop it over the side and pull it back up full. But don't lose it—or your arm."

A bucket of water returned. Oliver dipped the mop into it, wiped it over the port and starboard flukes, then tossed the whole bucket over the bow deck, turning the planking mud-gray.

"Hey Greg—can you get me another bucketful?"

Surprise had threaded her way out through the narrow entrance by the time the deck was clean again. Ahead lay Buzzards Bay, the same water he'd ambled across with Buck and Mrs. H—but now all he could see was line after line of breaking waves, tumbling white against the horizon. Now *that* looked like the Buzzards Bay from Cap'n Eli's stories.

Delivering cargo with Cap'n Eli! This was way better than listening to Mrs. Haverford tell Buck how it should–

"Look at that surf!" Greg pointed. "We can't go out there—it's way too rough. Didn't you see that movie *The Perfect Storm*? You're going to have to tell him–"

"Boy! Get that jumbo flying. Quick now."

Jumbo? That must be what Cap'n Eli called the staysail, the sail all the way forward on the bowsprit, the one Buck was too scared to use. Why not set the jib first?

Oliver crawled forward onto the netting, gripping hard with fingers and toes to keep from falling into the sea below–

"Jesus, Mary and Joseph—were you born in a barn? Not the jib! Jumbo always goes first."

Huh. So Cap'n Eli called the jib the "jumbo," and the staysail the "jib." How confusing.

Oliver and Greg hauled up the sail together and pulled the sheet in tight until it stopped luffing, just as Surprise nosed out into open water. The first wave over the bow drenched them both.

"Hey!" Greg yelled.

Oliver followed him back to the cockpit, grabbing the lifelines to keep from stumbling.

"What's with the waves?" Greg asked, wiping water out of his eyes.

"Current's running against the wind, which always kicks up a fuss," Cap'n Eli explained. "Besides that we got leftover storm swell. It'll smooth out some once we get away from the Hole."

The log put it slightly differently.

NEVER FOUND WEEPECKET NUN IN THE BIGGEST WAVES EVER ON THIS MOTHER OF A BAY. SURPRISE HANDLED IT FINE BUT NOT A DRY CORNER LEFT ABOARD.

Waves washed down the deck, breaking right over the coaming and into the cockpit. Why had he even bothered cleaning the foredeck? The whole boat was getting a full wash down now—including his bunk, probably.

Oliver wedged himself against the back face of the cabin, trying to find somewhere to hide from the spray. Greg headed below but quickly scrambled back up on deck, holding his stomach. He settled in next to Oliver, thumb against teeth so he could chew on his cuticles. He might bite off an entire joint on the next bone-rattling slam of a wave.

Cap'n Eli stood slightly uphill of the wheel, fingers wrapped around the spoke facing up. Boots braced on the wood deck, he leaned and tilted as he steered over each breaking crest.

"New Bedford's right on the nose." He had to raise his voice to be heard. "Only fourteen miles, but we're probably only doing about four knots."

"What's that mean?" Greg asked. He must be wishing he had a waterproof case for his MP3 player.

"Right on the nose? Dead upwind," Cap'n Eli replied. "So we have to tack to get there. Back and forth, like going up a steep hill on a bicycle. Not the best angle for Surprise, especially with these cussed–"

The next wave stopped her dead. Shuddering, she heeled over

a bit extra and gathered speed again.

"Might be better on port tack," Cap'n Eli said. "Hard-a-lee!"

"Need me to—"

Eli had already turned the helm toward the wind and eased the mainsheet a few feet. After a careful shrug, Surprise settled in again, leaning toward the opposite rail.

The motion was better, since they weren't sailing right into the waves. But after a few short minutes of relative comfort, Cap'n Eli shook his head.

"No good—now we're heading away from New Bedford. Hard-a-lee!"

A wave caught Surprise's bow just as she tacked, tossing it back into the cockpit. Oliver shook his hair dry—

"Hey!" Greg raised a hand to block his face. "Keep it to yourself, will you? I'm wet enough already."

If Cap'n Eli decided to leave Greg on the dock in New Bedford, that would be just fine.

12

~

HALF-DOZING AGAINST THE AFT FACE of the cabin, Oliver wrapped his arms around himself to keep warm. Every wave that sloshed down his neck seemed to murmur the words from the log. *"Not a dry corner left, not a dry corner left..."*

The biggest ones splashed into the cockpit and sometimes, right over his head. His bunk was probably sopping wet by now. Bashing upwind was a whole lot less fun than imagining it from a cozy armchair in his mother's office.

By late afternoon, this slamming wet world felt like all he'd ever known. Forearms and knees were crispy with sunburn, and both his eyes stung so much from the salt it was easier to keep them closed. So he wasn't quite sure what to think when he first felt the motion ease.

Pushing Greg off his left arm, he blinked over the cabin top. Ahead, green hills rolled up to a strange flare-topped tower.

"See the radome, boy? It's not far now—we'll be tied up before dark." Cap'n Eli winked one salt-whitened eyelid shut. "That wasn't so bad, was it? Now that it's almost over."

Flat water and the smell of gasoline greeted them in the wide channel. On the shoreline to port, huge tree rootballs stuck up into the air where the trunks should be. Every house had a hole in the roof or a busted window or something else wrong, and one had disappeared completely under a pine tree. No wonder his dad trimmed back branches all the time.

To starboard, one schooner lay on top of a second, bow merged into the other's stern.

"The Nonnie P." Cap'n Eli pointed to the one on top. Her two masts had washed ashore first, tangling in the only tree still standing. The rudder was jammed all the way to port on a nasty rock.

Eli shook his wet curls. "I hope Cap'n Rich is okay."

Silently they tacked into the harbor, the breeze dropping off with sunset just like any normal day. Every inch of shoreline had a dock, and every dock had a boat alongside—though some were half underwater.

Cap'n Eli heaved a huge sigh. "Guess we're not tying up in my usual spot. Drop sails!"

Greg headed forward to take care of the jumbo, so Oliver dropped the mainsail. Each halyard was made fast with a few wraps around its own belaying pin, a fat tapered dowel of wood dropped into a hole in the rail—but without the labels Mrs. H had added. Hopefully the layout hadn't changed. Oliver cast off two lines, and craned his neck to watch the sail come down. A bit faster on the throat…that's it. The sail dropped in a scatter of canvas. No lazy jacks, so he'd have to collect it all on top of the boom before he could get a gasket around it.

Eli turned to starboard, toward the only open stretch of pier. It didn't look quite long enough, and there was just a narrow walkway around the buildings, but it was the only choice.

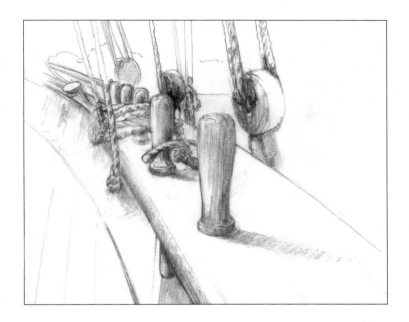

After ghosting the last hundred yards they tied up in silence, stern hanging out into the empty channel. Cap'n Eli stomped below as if he couldn't bear to see anymore.

"Look at that boat." Greg pointed to port. A schooner about the same size as Surprise had taken a bite out of the dock, bow in the air like she was climbing a wave even bigger than the ones they'd seen this morning.

Ashore the brick buildings had plywood over all the windows. And the dirt road leading away from the head of the dock was deserted—except for a small fishing boat, leaning against a telephone pole like it was waiting for a bus.

After another round of chowder Oliver fell into his bunk, salt-coated skin chafing against the damp mattress. What he wouldn't do for a fresh-water shower, a dry bunk—and a clean pair of pajamas.

He woke to feet stomping across the deck overhead. Skylight and companionway glowed with early morning.

Scrambling up the ladder, he spotted Cap'n Eli's curly head striding up the road. Across the dock, the top of the sun had already cracked the horizon.

He'd just filled the kettle when he heard a woman's voice.

"Ahoy Surprise!"

Scrambling up the ladder again, Oliver craned his neck right into the sun—couldn't be!

"Mom?" Before the word was even out of his mouth he wanted it back. He stumbled out into the cockpit, shading his eyes for a better view.

The girl on the dock was about his age, her plain white T-shirt dangling loose over pants rolled to her knees.

"You wish I was your mother." Her left eyebrow cocked up in a vee. "Where's Cap'n Eli?"

"He probably went to find someone to unload."

"Tough to get help today. Whole town's a shambles since Carol came to visit."

"Carol?"

"The hurricane, stupid! Remember how they started giving 'em girls' names last year?"

"Oh—yeah, of course."

"This one was a doozie—biggest one since '38, they're saying. Everyone's busy pulling trees off their houses or getting boats off the rocks. Probably have to–"

"Unload ourselves. Good idea, Liza." Cap'n Eli came around the corner of the nearest building. "What the devil are you doing here?"

Her gaze dropped to clenched fists. "I'm looking for a job, sir."

"A job! Don't you think you should be home taking care of your moth–" he stopped. "Nellie's gone, is she?"

"Two days ago." She let out a sigh so big it must've taken up her whole body. "I felt bad leaving Pa, especially with baby Josie to look after. But he just assumed I'd take over all the housework! I figured I'd help you with a cargo or two, until he works out how to cope without me. Whaddya say?"

Nellie, Josie. His grandmother, and his mom.

"I'm so sorry for your loss." Eli's automatic words ran together. "But I'm also glad your Ma is out of her pain at last."

He rested a square hand on the shoulder of Eliza's T-shirt. She rubbed a fist across her eyes.

They stood there a moment, until Cap'n Eli patted her shoulder once more and dropped his hand.

"Your timing's perfect, Eliza Nell. Looks like we need help unloading these cussed quayhogs. Ain't hardly ladies' work–"

"Crikey, Cap'n Eli! If I was scared of a little dirt I'd a gone somewhere else."

Eliza Nell.

Of course—Mom's oldest sister! Crazy Aunt Eliza, Mom called her, the tomboy sailor who'd run off right after Grandma Nellie died. No wonder she looked so familiar—especially when her eyebrow cocked up into that vee.

Now her twinkling eyes danced right past Oliver—to the shaggy head in the companionway.

"And what's your name?" Eliza placed one hand on her hip, like a movie star in canvas pants.

"Greg. Greg Haverford. Ah—ma'am." Greg's mouth hung open like he'd latched onto an electric fence.

"Ma'am! How old do you think I am?" The corners of her mouth turned down just like Mom's. "Where d'you hail from, Greg Haverford?"

"New Yo—"

"Greg's a castaway," Oliver interrupted. "He washed aboard Surprise just before..."

Nobody was listening.

Cap'n Eli jumped down onto the deck, crossing the high voltage line between Greg and Eliza.

"Jesus, Mary and Joseph, Greg—how many times have I told

you? Only admirals and admirals' bastards get to stand in the companionway."

Greg stepped up into the cockpit, his stupid open-mouthed grin still locked on Eliza.

Lifting up the creaking lazarette hatch, Cap'n Eli dragged out a thick black net. "I found a buyer," he said. "Three actually. They're up there right now, deciding who gets how many, and we gotta unload before they come to their senses." Gathering the net in his arms, he climbed down into the cabin. "Boy, unshackle the main halyard and pass it down to me."

Eliza balled up her yellow rain slicker and tossed it into the cockpit.

"Good thing you survived the storm, Cap'n Eli—plenty of work the next couple a days with so many boats on the beach. You hole up in Hadley's?"

There was no answer from below, and Greg's words had been shocked out of him.

She didn't even look at Oliver.

QUAHOG *A hard-shelled clam common to the waters around Cape Cod. One sixty pound bushel contains about eighty large quahogs.*

13

"HAUL AWAY!"

Oliver and Greg heaved on the main halyard, raising the black cargo net up through the companionway. It was lighter than Oliver expected, since the whole thing had to fit through the narrow hatch.

Cap'n Eli walked it across the deck, Oliver and Greg heaved again to raise it up to dock height, and once Eliza had grabbed it they lowered it down beside her. Dumping the four burlap bags neatly onto the dock, she passed the empty net back to Cap'n Eli.

"What a stink," Eliza said.

"Yeah, and he tried to get me to eat that poison," Greg told her.

"Only poison clams we ate were served by your—" Oliver stopped.

Greg looked away. Yesterday's sun had darkened his pasty white skin, but Oliver could tell he was blushing too.

"One more load from down here!" Cap'n Eli called. "Haul—"

"Greetings, little lady. Where's the captain?"

Three men in black overcoats and hats stood on the dock next to Eliza. The outside two could've been brothers—burly bookends to the skinny one in the middle. Greg stopped pulling, leaving Oliver barely hanging onto the halyard.

"Hey—I need help." Oliver gasped. Greg grabbed the halyard again, though his eyes remained on the men.

"I said, haul away!"

Another slightly larger netful of burlap slithered up through the companionway.

Cap'n Eli followed it on deck, nodding when he saw the men. Once the second load was safe in Eliza's hands, he smiled up at the three.

"So—you've decided?"

They must be the buyers.

Kneeling down next to the burlap bags, the right hand brother gave a loud sniff.

"Dug just a few days ago," Cap'n Eli told him. "From the sweetest flats on all of Nantucket, and kept perfectly cool ever since. The stink is from the seaweed they were packed in—you won't get 'em any fresher."

"This all you got?" the man asked.

"Hell no, that's just a start! Cargo hold's full."

Greg groaned. Oliver whacked him on the arm.

The skinny man nodded once. "We'll take everything you got, for ninety a pound."

Cap'n Eli snorted. "I'm not renting 'em to you."

The left bookend spoke. "None of the other New York buyers made it up here today. So we's the only ones buyin', on account a the storm."

"And I'm the only one selling—on account a the storm."

The three men stared down at Cap'n Eli. He twitched his shoulders into a careless shrug.

"Got a standing offer from Clem Saunders up at the Harbor

Restaurant—buck fifty a pound. You don't match his price, I'll drag the whole lot up there myself."

"One ten," the skinny man responded.

"One forty," Cap'n Eli fired back.

"One twenty-five."

"Sold." Eli reached up to shake each hand in turn. "We'll get the rest of 'em unloaded in a jiffy. Have your truck here in, say, forty minutes?"

After a curt nod from the skinny guy the three men strode away, coats flapping.

"You really think there's more?" Greg asked. "My arms're falling off already."

Cap'n Eli slid back a large hatch between the mainmast and the cabin, letting out a now familiar salty stench. Scrambling down the short ladder, he called for the net to be lowered down behind him. After filling it with as many bags as it would hold, he nodded up at Oliver.

"Haul away!"

Five, eight, ten loads... Oliver soon stopped counting. As the heap on the dock grew, his arms and back burned. He was breathing hard, too—but so was Greg.

At last Cap'n Eli climbed out of the empty hold.

"That's the last of it. How many've we got, Liza?"

She grunted, finger moving from one burlap bag to the next. Greg called back first. "Ninety-two."

Cap'n Eli closed his eyes. "I'll throw in the open bushel. Sixty pounds each, times one twenty-five…" He smiled. "That'll be a tidy profit, especially since we unloaded ourselves. Almost as good as the old days. I wonder–"

"Ahoy Surprise!" A tall man in a dark suit peered over the edge of the dock. "Well, if it ain't Cap'n Eli."

"Expecting someone else, Mr. Ellis?" Climbing back down the short ladder, Cap'n Eli began to heave leftover seaweed out of the hold. A few dried-out strands rode the northwesterly breeze up toward the dock.

Waving a piece away from his face, Mr. Ellis curled his lips into a smile. "Survived the storm, I see."

"Holed up in Hadley's, snug as a bug," Cap'n Eli replied. "Yours come through all right?"

The man shook his head, though his oiled hair never moved. "Cap'n Jack did a runner. Sarah Ann tore herself and the other side of this dock apart. She'll probably be laid up for good."

"He left her—on her own?"

"Yes indeed. Proof's right over there." Mr. Ellis pointed a long finger past the dock building to a pair of broken-off masts, heeling against pilings that weren't so straight either. "Jack Ames'll never work for me again."

"How 'bout the Becky Ann?"

"She left a week ago, bound for Long Island. I was expecting her back by now."

"She'll turn up. Harris is a wily old coot."

"Not as wily as you—the only coaster still running under sail, making the first delivery since the storm! Bet you named your price for those clams, even though they smell like they've been aboard awhile."

Cap'n Eli went back to his seaweed-pitching.

Ellis shifted his gaze to Eliza. "Mighty nice of you to help unload, young lady."

Eliza pressed her lips together.

"Liza's just signed on as my mate," Cap'n Eli said.

"Mate—well, fancy that! What do these other two think about that? This one looks like he could sail the boat all by himself." Mr. Ellis winked at Oliver.

"That's my ship's boy." Cap'n Eli waved a meaty hand toward Greg. "And this one's working his way back to the Cape."

Mr. Ellis fingered the end of his bow tie.

"I've a cargo for Vineyard Haven," he said. "I'll pay you a bonus if it's delivered by tomorrow."

Cap'n Eli didn't reply.

"And I'll pay you another bonus to leave your pretty mate ashore." Mr. Ellis' gaze shifted back to Eliza. "Since I wouldn't want your great luck to change."

"Pah!" Cap'n Eli spat to his left. "Old wives' tales—Liza's one of the best."

"I don't hold with women on my boats."

"Surprise ain't one of your boats," Eli replied.

"Even for a double bonus?"

"Nope."

"Humph! I'll guess I'll take my business elsewhere."

Leaning on the shovel, Cap'n Eli's lips stretched taut. "Ayuh, thought you might."

Eliza's gaze followed Mr. Ellis' dark suit back up the dock.

"I just cost us a cargo!"

Scrambling up out of the hold, Cap'n Eli swatted away a stray piece of seaweed that had stuck to his trousers. "Oh I could've talked him round, Liza. But I'll run empty before I carry anything of his. Notice how he never said what his precious cargo actually was? Whenever something stinks he's never far away. And I don't mean seaweed stink."

He looked up at the head of the dock, visible from Surprise's deck now that she'd lifted on the incoming tide.

"And if a man who's never spared one word for me is talking double bonuses, there'll be plenty of other cargoes."

Crossing to the bottom of the ladder, Cap'n Eli stopped.

"No point in all of you standing around while I'm off collecting our pay. Boy, you get that seaweed back over the side where it belongs. Liza, there's a couple hanks on the jumbo that need a new lashing. And Greg—hmm, what can you do?"

"I'll help Liza."

"Long as you mind her—none of your guff, now."

"With pleasure." When Greg smiled, his face lit up like a soundstage.

"I'll go collect that clam money. And then I'll figure out where we're headed next." Scrabbling up the ladder, Cap'n Eli strode off again, rubber boots crunching gravel underfoot.

After pitching most of the seaweed over the side, Oliver pulled the metal bucket out of the lazarette. He was about to drop it over the side when Eliza stopped him.

"Don't put that filthy harbor water on a clean deck! Grab some fresh, from up on the dock."

She was right—the harbor *was* filthy. A small piece of wood swirled by in an oily eddy, followed by a long tail of wood shavings and sawdust. Ashore, Oliver saw a man walking back up from the water's edge with an empty can. A woodshop, probably, tossing their trash into the harbor. Yuck.

So he dragged the bucket up the short stretch of ladder, hoping he wouldn't get a splinter from the wooden rungs.

Might as well take a look at the schooner on the other side, while he was here. The Sarah Ann, was it? One of the names in Eli's log.

Gravel dug into the soles of his feet as he crossed the dock. And once he saw her, he wished he'd stayed away. The white hull was crushed where she'd bashed against a piling, and most of the rigging hung slack down into the water. Surprise had never looked this banged up, even when she was rotting away at his mom's yard. So sad.

He hobbled back across to where water spouted from a busted pipe. After trying to fill the bucket from the undirected spray (and rinsing off most of his own salt), he turned on the faucet instead. The water tasted as sweet as a water fountain.

Back at the edge of the dock, he eased the full bucket down onto the deck and glanced forward. Eliza sat on the jumbo boom, sawing a knife across the lashing that attached a metal clip to the sail. Greg knelt right beside her, waiting, a needle and long piece of waxed twine in one hand and a leather sailmaker's palm in the other.

Sighing, Oliver jumped down onto the deck. It would be really cool to get to know Aunt Eliza. But he wasn't going to fight his way past Greg to—

Liza, Cap'n Eli called her. She must be the Liza from the ship's log! Huh—if he'd realized the name referred to his crazy long-lost aunt, he would've paid more attention.

By the time Cap'n Eli returned, all the seaweed was gone. Oliver had even scrubbed around the cargo hatch and back to the cockpit.

"I see you're not afraid of hard work."

"Doesn't feel like work, sir."

"Even better." Cap'n Eli squatted on his haunches beside the companionway. "I found a load of bricks that needs to get over to Woods Hole. One of them semi trucks was supposed to take 'em, but it ain't here yet. So we can deliver the bricks and Greg too." He pulled at his right earlobe. "Load's bigger than we're used to. We'll have to put some in the cabin…" he stared down through the opening.

"If you need my bunk I can sleep on—"

Cap'n Eli laughed. "Keep your bunk, boy. Gotta stack the heavy stuff down low, keep her feet under her. That's why I don't want to put any more on deck than we have to." He stood up again, ankles creaking.

"Let's try four pallets below." He smoothed down the top of his curls, but they popped right back up again. "Like old times, wondering whether a whole cargo'll fit onboard. And still only one way to find out."

14

THE BRICKS WERE LOADED ONTO Surprise the same way the clams left—by Oliver and Greg heaving on a halyard. The pallets weren't that big, but each was a solid cube of red—ten bricks long, ten wide, and three high. Three hundred bricks, times—what did a brick weigh? All Oliver knew is that each pallet was way harder to lift than a cargo net full of clams.

They lost control of the first one lowering it into the hold and it landed with an echoing thunk, like it had blasted a hole right through the hull. Good thing Surprise was so tough.

Eli rigged a short tackle for more purchase and Eliza tied a line to the side of the next pallet, easing it out until the bricks were right over the opening. Once they established a rhythm, pallets disappeared into the hold until it was so full Cap'n Eli had to back up the ladder. And there was still a stack on the dock.

The next four pallets went down into the cabin. The last eight stacked on deck, covering the cargo hatch and filling up the open deck aft of the mainmast. Cap'n Eli ran a web of lines to keep the stacks from shifting underway.

Next he handed Oliver the end of a black hose and asked him to connect it to the faucet on the dock.

"Water tastes better in Woods Hole, but that won't matter if we run out before we get there."

Huh! So Cap'n Eli did drink something other than rain water.

After several minutes Cap'n Eli shouted, "Shut 'er off!" Oliver coiled the hose, stashed it back in the lazarette, and climbed down into the cabin. Eli knelt forward of the tank, gripping the rusty screwdriver.

"Lost a lot of water into the bilge the past year—this clamp seems to loosen up now whenever the tank's topped off. I tried replacing it but that didn't make any difference. So now I just tighten it up every time—there."

Sliding the floorboard back into place, he nodded at the bricks stacked behind the companionway ladder. "Full tank of water, a full cargo hold, and a perfect breeze! What could be—"

"Cap'n Eli?" Eliza called down the companionway, tilting her dark hair toward the dock. "There's a boy asking for you."

He was small and shirtless, but he tipped his cap like a tiny gentleman. "Heard you was headed across the Bay today, sir?"

"I am." Cap'n Eli frowned. "You're Cap'n Rich's boy, aren't you—off the Nonnie P? Saw her on the beach. He all right?"

The boy shook his head. "He tried to get her out to sea when the storm hit, but she got blown up on the beach. His leg's broke bad."

"Damn shame—good man, he is."

"Yes, sir," the boy nodded. "He was hopin' you might have room to take some Rhode Island Reds to Woods Hole."

"I guess so," Cap'n Eli replied. "They don't weigh much, anyway."

"Thanks, Cap'n Eli—I'll go tell the driver to bring 'em down. When d'you leave?"

"On the ebb, which must be pretty soon." Cap'n Eli glanced back at the companionway, forehead wrinkling. "That cussed clock's stopped again."

"Ebb's in a half hour," the boy replied. "I'll tell 'em to hurry."

"Best to Cap'n Rich, hear?"

The boy scurried away, bare ankles and feet sticking out below wool pants.

"Jaysus to jaysus." Cap'n Eli rubbed one hand across the blond stubble on his chin. "Where we gonna put chickens?"

There was only one place the cages would fit—on top of the bricks. Oliver had just tied down the last squawking bird when a deep voice boomed over from the dock.

"Found a nice fresh cargo, heh heh," Mr. Ellis cackled. "I just hope you can hear yourself think over all that racket."

"We'll be fine," Cap'n Eli replied. "And if this northerly holds, we'll be in Woods Hole quick as a thought."

But by the time they cast off, the northerly had faded off to nothing. They drifted away from the dock with the beginning of the ebb.

"Four lowers, Liza." Cap'n Eli had to shout to be heard above the birds.

"Aye sir." She headed to the bow.

Mainsail, foresail, jumbo, jib, Oliver said to himself. He helped Greg haul up the main which felt like nothing after all those bricks, and then he headed forward to raise the foresail. He had to climb up between the chicken cages to untie the gaskets, trying not to think of all those tiny beaks within pecking distance of his ankles–

This wouldn't work. The cages stacked up higher than the boom, so once the sail was let out it would sweep the chickens overboard.

"Ah, Cap'n Eli?"

Turning the wheel over to Eliza, Cap'n Eli strode forward.

"So long since we carried a tall load, I forgot one thing." He pointed to a second bronze plate with two vertical holes on the aft side of the mast. "We have to raise the boom up to cargo height so it can swing out over the chickens."

"Oh—I see."

Untying the throat halyard, Cap'n Eli secured it around the inboard end of the boom, which set off a fresh round of squawking.

"Lift the boom just enough to take the weight, and I'll get the pin out—that's plenty." Eli pulled out the bronze rod, thick as his thumb and twice as long.

"Now raise her up, boy—too much! Ease a hair... a little more—there." Lining up the boom with the higher gooseneck, Cap'n Eli dropped the pin into its new home. "Now we can set the foresail without sending any chickens overboard. For all the good it'll do us, in this calm." He glanced back at the dock. "Good to be off, anyway, away from that damned Mr. Ellis. These hens are noisy, but at least they're not trying to talk me into a shady deal."

Oliver handed off the foresail peak halyard to Greg and pulled up the throat halyard. Under her four drooping lowers, Surprise drifted out of the harbor with the fair current. Eliza handled the wheel like she'd been steering Surprise her whole life, leaving channel marks closer than Oliver would've dared and even going inside a small white spar buoy.

By the time they reached the open waters of Buzzards Bay, even the chickens had mostly quieted down.

"There's Woods Hole Pass." Cap'n Eli pointed across the glassy Bay to a low spot between two green humps. "Just keep her going toward that, best you can."

Surprise lifted over the first gentle wave, the extra weight of the bricks thickening her motion. She seemed as happy as Cap'n Eli to be carrying a full cargo. Oliver was happy too, though his growling stomach reminded him they'd missed both breakfast and lunch. Even a cold Johnnycake would taste pretty good.

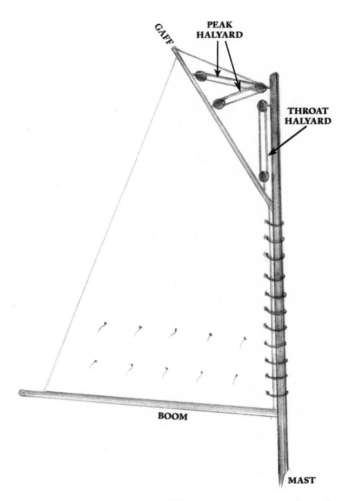

Fortunately Cap'n Eli set a fishing line as soon as they cleared the channel. When the line whizzed over the transom, he hauled in a nice fat cod.

"I'll clean it," Greg offered. "My dad taught me how on our last camping trip."

"All yours then." Cap'n Eli pulled out the hook and handed over the fish, which was still smacking its tail back and forth. "Just make sure you scrub the deck down after. Fish guts leave a nasty stain."

Greg carved out two neat fillets, dropping them into the metal pan Eliza passed up from the galley. Soon after the mouth-watering scent of frying fish curled up through the skylight, Eliza handed up two full plates and two overflowing bowls.

"Tie off the wheel and join us, Cap'n Eli."

The fish was delicious. Greg must've agreed, since he emptied his bowl even sooner than Oliver.

"Nothing melts in your mouth like Buzzards Bay cod." Setting down her fork, Eliza looked aft. "Where'd you put the rest of the fish, Greg?"

"Uh… I threw it overboard."

"You—crikey, what a waste!" She smacked a palm against the side of her head. "I coulda made a chowder. And now some other fish'll get the cheeks."

"Cod cheeks—pah." Cap'n Eli spat to his right. "Supposed to be such a delicacy. To me they taste just like the rest of the damn fish, only smaller."

"I can catch another one–"

"That's not the point—it's a waste of good food. My Pa would take you across his knee, big as you are." Still shaking her head, Eliza carried the dishes below to wash up.

Greg caught Oliver's eye and shrugged, though his cheeks had reddened again. Eliza sure got territorial quick about the cooking and cleaning, which seemed strange when that was what she'd run away from home to avoid.

Back on the helm, Cap'n Eli whistled an aimless tune. Beckoning Greg out of the companionway, Oliver led him by the sleeve all the way to the bow. Before Greg could say anything, Oliver shook a finger in front of his face.

"Stay away from Eliza," he growled. "She's way too old for you."

"No way—how do you figure that?"

"She was born in 1940! That makes her almost seventy in our time."

"She's not seventy right now. Did you check out her butt? I never thought canvas pants could curve like—"

"Shut up! I'm serious."

"So am I." Greg glared at him.

Crossing arms over his crusty T-shirt, Oliver glared back.

"How do you know what year she was born?" Greg asked.

"She's my aunt."

"No way! Why doesn't she recognize you?"

"We've never met. She ran away to sea when my mom was just a baby. Baby Josie." Oliver hauled in a ragged breath. "And besides, you and I haven't been born yet, remember? She can't recognize someone who doesn't exist."

"Woh." Greg rubbed the back of one hand against the black fuzz of his chin. "This is just way too weird."

"Yeah."

"How'd you get back to the right time, last time?"

"When the hurricane hit, I passed out again."

"Again?"

"That's how I first went back in time. I fell down the companionway ladder."

"It is kind of steep—think we should try that?"

Oliver shook his head. "It seems like you have to go back the same way you came."

"No way—I am NOT eating bad clams again!" Greg's hands went to his belly. "And how do we scare up another hurricane?"

"I don't know." Oliver sighed. "But we definitely need to get back to Hadley's."

Greg kicked the heel of his sneaker against the windlass.

"What if—only one of us makes it back?"

"No clue. Last time it was just me."

"Shoot, I'd go completely bonkers if I were here by myself." Greg's eyes wandered aft, following Eliza as she joined Cap'n Eli at the wheel. "Sure you're not just jealous?"

"Jeez, Greg! I'm too young to be thinking like that. And she is too—she's only fourteen."

"First you say she's too old, and now she's too young? Sure sounds like you're jealous. I think she—"

Oliver's punch—his first, ever—missed. But it caught the side of Greg's head, and since Greg's hands were stuffed deep in his pockets, he stumbled back over the windlass and fell to the deck.

"Man—what'd you do that for?"

"Greg! Are you hurt?" Eliza ran forward and knelt down, stroking black bangs out of his eyes.

Greg's face had crumpled into a sulk but her words wiped it clean.

"Let me up," he growled. "I've got to defend myself."

"Boy! Come back here." Cap'n Eli's right arm lifted off the wheel to wave him aft.

Oliver shuffled back to Cap'n Eli.

"Sorry, sir. I didn't mean to hit him."

"Don't apologize—the kid's a brat. You shoulda left him to drown in Hadley Harbor." Cap'n Eli winked. "Now take over a spell, wouldja? I've gotta go pump my personal bilge."

CANS *Unlighted, flat-topped green buoys that are left to port, the left side. In 1980 the color was updated from black to green.*

15

ONCE HE TOUCHED THE WHEEL, Oliver forgot all about Greg and Eliza. Surprise talked to him through her helm, asking him to steer a little to port as the light breeze shifted, or a little to starboard to work through a wave. He'd wondered how Buck figured it out so fast, but now he understood—even with a belly full of bricks, Surprise knew what she wanted.

Cap'n Eli reappeared and crossed to the weather rail to study the Bay ahead, a curly-topped silhouette against reddening sky. Oliver couldn't see their wake, but he liked to think it was as straight as Buck's. If Cap'n Eli didn't agree, he'd have to order Oliver off the helm.

After sunset the breeze died off to nothing. They drifted into the open bight outside Hadley's, and since the current in the Hole was against them they dropped sail and anchored right there. Cap'n Eli went below to catch "some shuteye."

Oliver stayed on deck, partly to watch the stars but mostly to keep the cockpit from becoming a love nest. Didn't matter—Greg and Eliza settled down on the foredeck. Oliver couldn't see anything past the chickens, but he heard an occasional throaty laugh—just like Mom's.

The moon crept across the sky, back toward New Bedford. Tiny waves slapped at the skiff as Surprise swung to her anchor. And an annoying silence fell, up on the foredeck.

His eyes were closing on their own...

CLANG!

Jeez, what was that? Something heavy must've crashed below.

He'd forgotten about the chickens, but now they started squawking again. Oliver uncurled his stiff body and peered forward into the dark, trying to see the foredeck.

Cap'n Eli came on deck chuckling.

"Don't you worry about Liza, boy. Anyone who can keep out of trouble on the New Bedford docks for two days can handle a brat with a fancy wristwatch."

"She was there for two days?"

"Ayuh, waiting for Surprise. Left home the day her ma died. Rest in peace, Nellie-Bell." He sighed. "I think after this cargo I'll head home. You ever meet Mr. Nichols?"

He's my grandfather, Oliver wanted to reply. Instead he shrugged.

"No reason why you should've—everything on Narragansett Bay moves by truck nowadays. Just like it will on the Cape, one day soon." He stretched his arms overhead. "But not tonight! We've got two cargoes, a nice bit of nor'west breeze, and the current's finally turned fair. Liza!" He called forward. "Get that anchor up."

He turned back to Oliver. "Like to steer her off, boy?"

"Yessir!"

"You'll have to be patient with her—she's a bear to handle before she gets her legs under her." He strode forward.

"Greg! Look lively—we'll haul up the main soon as Liza's got the anchor started."

"Ready here, sir," she called, just as the steady clank of windlass began.

"How did I ever sail this fine schooner by myself?" Crooked teeth shining in the moonlight, Cap'n Eli handed the peak halyard off to Greg. "Pull even with me now. Heave—ho. Heave—ho."

The main and its heavy gaff crept up the mast, but Surprise's helm remained silent. Seemed like everyone was busy, except Oliver.

"Ease–that–main–sheet." Cap'n Eli spoke in rhythm with his massive halyard pulls.

Oliver let out ten feet of worn line, past the fat bump of a splice. The boom crept off to starboard.

"One more—heave. That's it." Tying off the two halyards, Cap'n Eli turned back to Oliver. "Ease that main right out, so she'll turn for you without a headsail. Wheel hard to starboard."

Oliver spun the wheel and held it. The bow began to respond, the mainsail filled, and soon he felt the tug on the helm— Surprise was talking again. *Rudder only works when there's water flowing over it,* he heard Buck repeat in his head. He pictured the large wooden blade underwater, the water flowing by, and his skin tingled. Now it all made sense!

A shout from Eliza in the bow.

"Head up a bit, slow her down," Eli said. "Doesn't hurt to drag the anchor and clean the mud off, but we don't want to drive it up into the hull."

Oliver let the wheel return two spokes to port. Nothing happened, so he let it spin back to neutral. Now she was turning too fast—she would go into irons if he didn't stop her. Before Cap'n Eli could say anything he quickly spun three, four, five spokes to starboard—and Surprise came down so fast again he could hear the anchor clank against the hull. That's how boats got holed! Heart pounding, he gently moved the helm one spoke back to port and counted to five, slowly. The course steadied out.

"That's it, lad." Cap'n Eli was right beside him again. "Gotta wait for her to respond when she's loaded so—"

"Anchor's up," Eliza called.

"Now you can bear off."

Cap'n Eli eased the mainsheet until the boom hovered out over moonlit water, perpendicular to the black hull. When he steered he also trimmed the huge sail himself. Oliver couldn't concentrate on anything but the wheel.

"See our first channel mark?" Cap'n Eli's stubby finger pointed just off the port bow.

Oliver peered across at the black lump of Penzance Point. Something squatted low in the water—could that be a buoy? Less than half the size he expected.

When a shaft of moonlight landed on it, he was sure— the miniature red cone already leaned east. And just off the starboard bow was that big pile of square granite blocks, its tower a rusty web against the stars.

Eliza came aft, rubbing the mud off her hands. "Anchor's stowed, Cap'n Eli. Want me to take over?" Greg had waited for her by the mainmast, and now he followed a few steps behind.

"We'll let the boy con her through the Hole. Hoist the jumbo, and sheet her in on centerline."

"Let the boy—" she stopped. "Aye, sir." Eliza spun forward again, Greg following behind like a faithful retriever.

Cap'n Eli chuckled again. Oliver was too busy replaying his words to ask what he was laughing about. He'd get to steer all the way through the Hole! Even in daylight so many things could happen.

"Ah, sir—"

"I'm right here, boy. And Surprise knows what to do. Head for the rock pile now—that'll get you centered up."

Oliver turned a spoke to starboard, feeling the boat slow down as the apparent wind dropped. This wasn't so different from the sailing he did at home, except Surprise and her heavy cargo took so long to answer her helm. No wonder the insurance company wanted an engine back in her.

"Wish I'd woke up a half hour sooner," Cap'n Eli muttered. "Gotta refine that tide alarm. I like going through when the current's still just against us—everything happens slower."

The main boom pulsed in a few feet. With the current and wind both pushing from astern, there was not enough pressure to keep the large sail filled.

"Jumbo's set, sir," Eliza reported.

"Good. Now hold that main boom out."

Eliza raised her arms overhead, white T-shirt glowing in the moonlight, and pushed the heavy wooden spar out as far as it would go. Greg pushed too, though you could barely see his black outline. Slowly and yet too fast Surprise crept toward the rock pile, until they were close enough to see an osprey hunkered down in its spiked nest at the top of the tower. The bird's head cocked to one side, following their progress.

"Now head for the next nun. See it?"

Greg dropped his arms.

"Keep holding that boom!" Cap'n Eli bellowed.

Oliver turned the wheel one spoke to port.

"Used to sail her right over where that rockpile is, before they built it. Some treacherous on the other side. You can't tell how the current's gonna swirl around all the—steady!" Surprise 's wheel lurched to starboard, pulling Oliver sideways. Before he could recover Cap'n Eli reached out to spin the wheel to port.

"Feel that? Current's kicking against the rudder. You gotta answer quick or we'll end up on the rocks."

Heart pounding, Oliver forced his hands down by his sides, away from the wheel. What did Eli expect? The Hole wasn't the place to learn how to steer a big schooner.

Cap'n Eli glanced over at him. "Go on, take her back. Can't learn without making a mistake or two along the way."

So Oliver placed each hand on a spoke again, spreading his feet wide to brace for the next unexpected current eddy.

Another red nun danced past, its cone-shaped top barely visible above the swirling water.

Cap'n Eli pointed again.

"There's the next one. Leave it close to port."

Where?

Thanks to the moon, he caught a glimpse of another nun just before it rushed by. The tide—current—was really starting to rip.

"Good. Now line up Grassy Island with the bow of the ferry and keep that bearing steady." His hand dropped briefly onto Oliver's shoulder.

The red and white spindle had been knocked over backward. Oliver wanted to check it out, but he had to concentrate. Safely past the last buoy, he started to turn to—

"Not yet!" Cap'n Eli held up his hand. "Remember the rock that steps out into the channel."

Buck's rock.

"Steady—okay, now you can head up." Cap'n Eli trimmed in the mainsheet, hand over meaty hand.

"Spot the harbor marker yet?" Cap'n Eli peered over the port rail into the darkness. "Hard to see, black can against black water."

"Green, isn't it sir?"

"Cans are black. Though green'd be a helluva lot easier to see at night. Now where is that blasted—ah, there it is, the little she-devil. We'll tack just before we hit the ferry dock. That'll give us enough room to clear the can, even with the current coming out of the harbor." He raised his voice to carry forward. "Jumbo full and by, Eliza."

Oliver felt the wheel pressure lighten under his palms.

"That better?" Cap'n Eli nodded. "She do like a balanced helm."

Just ahead, the ferry stood huge and white against the dark land. It seemed like the bowsprit was just about to ram into it when Cap'n Eli finally nodded.

"Okay, lad. Three spokes to port. Hard-alee!"

"Aye, sir." Spinning the wheel, he felt the schooner hesitate, white sails shaking overhead, before she fell off onto starboard tack.

"Full and by, sir," Eliza reported. "We tyin' up tonight?"

"No. We'll anchor off, tie up in daylight."

The small can was definitely black, and once it slid by the port rail Cap'n Eli asked Greg to let go the jumbo halyard. It came down in a heap, unbalancing the rudder so Oliver had to turn a half spoke to port.

Jumbo furled, Cap'n Eli spoke again.

"Two spokes to starboard, boy—head her right into the wind."

Surprise crept forward, mainsail luffing. Nosing into the empty harbor, she gradually lost way through the shining water, slower still, until–

"Drop anchor!"

Eliza let the chain run, and Oliver stood at the now useless wheel while Cap'n Eli let the main halyards go. What a rush, steering Surprise through the Hole! Especially when the current pushed her sideways and he'd thought–

"Boy! Snug up that mainsheet and then help me with this cussed sail. Bring two more gaskets."

Oliver climbed onto the cabin top and began to pull at the tough canvas, laying one fold on top of the other so Cap'n Eli could get a sail tie around the whole mess.

"Ever thought of rigging lazy jacks, sir?"

"I'd never trust anything with the word lazy in it." Cap'n Eli knotted the first gasket tight.

"They're just lines that run from the mast down to the boom.

Keeps the sail together until you can get it tied up."

"Where'd you see those?"

"Oh, I don't know." Oliver shrugged, feeling his face heat up. "Just thought of it, I guess."

"Jaysus, where d'you get all these crazy ideas? Green cans and lazy lines. You'll have to draw me a–"

"Anchor's holding, sir." Eliza grabbed an elbow in each hand. "Okay if I turn in?"

"Go ahead, mate Eliza." He watched her climb below, then turned forward. "Greg? Need a word."

"Yeah—ah, yes, sir."

"You'll stand the first anchor watch. If you even think anything's wrong, wake me right away. I sleep with one eye open anyway."

"Aye aye, sir."

Oliver thought Greg was gonna salute.

Once they were done wrestling the main into a neat sausage, Cap'n Eli headed below too.

"So what do we do now?" Greg whispered. "We sailed right past Hadley's."

Oliver whispered back. "This might take a little longer than we thought."

Greg's pale skin had darkened with the sun, and a few freckles dotted his cheeks. "You should be happy to have more time with your new girlfriend," Oliver told him.

"She doesn't seem to like me that much after all."

"She's just not as loose as you're used to."

"That's for sure." Greg shook his mane of hair. "And I guess I'm not doing a very good job of fitting in. She said I look like a girl."

Oliver grinned, suddenly. "Smart girl, that Liza."

SEAL PEN *The Woods Hole Aquarium kept harbor seals just inside the seawall until 1954, when they escaped with the high waters of Hurricane Carol. Since 1960 two seals have frolicked in a small pool between the aquarium building and the street.*

16

~~~~~~

O LIVER WOKE JUST AFTER DAWN and stretched, touching either end of his bunk with hands and feet. He was almost asleep again when he heard a loud crash, followed by chickens squawking.

The same metal slam he'd heard in the middle of the night. What was it?

Cap'n Eli crawled out of his bunk scratching his right ear, and stepped into his boots on the cabin sole—right next to the frying pan. A small line stretched from the handle up the companionway ladder. Was that the tide alarm Cap'n Eli had talked about? How did it work? Oliver swung his feet out of his bunk and down onto the settee.

"Jesus, Mary and Joseph—wouldja look at that!"

Oliver had never seen Cap'n Eli stop short in the companionway before.

"The dock's gone."

"Gone?"

"Well, almost. Might as well be." Cap'n Eli climbed the rest of the way up the ladder like his boots were filled with lead.

Oliver peered out into the cockpit. Tucked in the aft corner, Greg rubbed at his eyes and angled his knees outboard to slide something shiny back into his pocket. Hopefully that battery was just about dead.

Behind Greg lay the town of Woods Hole, though it looked totally different. The brick aquarium had been replaced by a shingled place that looked like a huge summer home. Two long piers stepped out into the harbor in front of it, closing off a large basin. Or rather, they used to close it off—half the decking was gone. Now the basin looked like an open mouth with half its teeth knocked out.

Boats lay on their sides like driftwood around the horseshoe-shaped harbor. The tiny Yacht Club tilted north, and a boat heeled over in the parking lot.

And the town dock—Jeez! It had been pulled apart like an erector set after a tantrum. What had been a solid wharf was now a jumble of logs, lumber, and boats, not a place Surprise could lay alongside.

"I knew the storm would be bad here—harbor's wide open to the southeast. But I didn't think the whole dock'd be lost. Damnation!" Making a fist, Cap'n Eli whacked the cockpit coaming hard—so hard Oliver felt it in the planking beneath his feet. "Now we'll have to take these cussed bricks and chickens right back to—"

"We can row 'em ashore in the skiff," Oliver said.

"That would take forever!"

"They must be desperate for building supplies, with everything so trashed. Almost as desperate as we are to get rid of the chickens." They'd started squawking again when Cap'n Eli whacked the rail.

"Boy's right, sir." Eliza spoke from the companionway ladder behind Oliver. "If we take turns all four of us, it won't be too bad."

Cap'n Eli chewed on the inside of his cheek, then heaved a huge sigh.

"Better rustle us up some johnnycakes then," he told Eliza. "We'll need all our strength today."

After breakfast, Cap'n Eli pulled the skiff alongside Surprise and Oliver handed the squawking birds down to him. He stacked the cages three high.

"Now pull a few bricks off that pallet," Cap'n Eli said. "We'll all go ashore with the first load, see if anyone's paying enough to make it worth unloading the rest."

"I'll row," Greg offered.

"Okay then, let's see how you do," replied Cap'n Eli, taking a seat on the stern thwart.

It was a tough boat to handle—heavy, with a long skeg that made it hard to turn. But Greg couldn't even get both oars going in the same direction. After a few circles that set Eliza giggling, Cap'n Eli grabbed the oars and rowed back to Surprise. Eliza sat down next to a red-faced Greg in the wide stern, trying not to smile. Oliver perched on the forward thwart, knees pulled against his chest so he didn't kick the chicken cages.

Up close, the town dock looked even worse. Timbers half the length of Surprise pointed to the sky, no longer attached to their pilings. Two boats had sunk right where Surprise had tied up the last time. Their stubby masts shot up from below the surface like submarine antennas radioing for help.

Cap'n Eli rowed past the end of the dock into a small cove and around two capsized sailboats still attached to their moorings. Junk littered the beach, jumbled so thick the sand was hardly visible.

At the steep ramp, Oliver jumped out to tug the skiff as far as he could up the seaweedy concrete.

Eli stepped over the rail into shallow water. "I'll go find a spot we can dump these damned birds until—"

"Ahoy, Cap'n Eli!" A pot-bellied man in all khaki ambled

down to greet them. "You and Surprise made it through just fine, I see."

"Hello, Stanley." Eli shook the outstretched hand. "We tucked away in Hadley Harbor—don't know why more folks didn't join us. Your boat okay?"

"She's hauled out for a fresh coat of antifouling paint, thank the good Lord. Only now the boatyard's too busy with salvage work to get to it."

"Still, you're lucky." Cap'n Eli nodded to his right. "Good thing you weren't tied up here."

"I woulda headed offshore to ride it out, like everyone else except Matt and Gus." Stanley waved at the two sunken boats. "They probably told each other they'd be safe in the lee of the Fisheries docks, but waves were breaking right across the parking lot. One of the floating docks from the small boat basin broke free—that's what knocked the Yacht Club off its pins. Aquarium seals even escaped." The fat-knuckled finger pointing south was somehow familiar.

"What a shame." Cap'n Eli's grimace locked on the tallest mast, where a halyard dangled loose.

He turned back to Stanley.

"We brought a load of brick and these damned chickens over from New Bedford, but now we can't get alongside to unload. Is there a ship's boy who could watch 'em while we go ferry in the rest of—"

"Now first of all, those brooders belong to Louis Arnold over at Tsiknas' market." Stanley threw a thumb over his shoulder. "He stopped by yesterday afternoon and said you were bringin' 'em over, so I'm sure he'll be down with his truck any minute. As for the bricks..." Stanley leaned back on his heels, thumbs latched into belt loops. "Got a buyer?"

Eli shook his head. "Not yet. Original order was from a builder in Falmouth. I told the broker we was headed for Woods Hole, and I guess he figured that was close enough."

Oliver didn't dare make eye contact with Greg.

"I'm sure someone'll be wanting bricks, with all the damaged buildings." Stanley clapped Cap'n Eli on the shoulder. "Tell you what—I'll sit by what you bring in. Might even find a buyer."

"I'm happy to pay for–"

"Go on, Eli. You'd do the same for me."

For the first time that morning, Eli smiled. "Thanks a lot, Stanley."

Back on Surprise, Oliver shackled the block and tackle to the main halyard and hooked it into the top pallet closest to the skiff. He and Greg lowered the first one down, but after letting out a colorful string of cuss words Cap'n Eli told them to lift it back on deck—it was too long to fit between the two thwarts. They'd have to take each pallet apart, loading brick by endless brick.

Heaving a deep sigh, Cap'n Eli divided the jobs. Oliver would remove the wire that held the bricks together and then help Eliza hand the bricks down to the skiff. Greg and Cap'n Eli would row in, unload each stack, and row back out again. Good thing they got an early start—it would take all day, at least.

Oliver figured Greg'd start whining, but instead he outpaced Cap'n Eli. Maybe he was just showing off for Eliza, but he seemed to enjoy the repetitive work. And his fingers were so long, he could lift two bricks with one hand! Oliver couldn't manage more than one at a time.

After slicing his thumb, Oliver borrowed some canvas gloves—but they were too thick to work the pliers. Both palms were soon stinging with a web of cuts from the wire ends.

Once they cleared the deck, Oliver hopped down into the hold—where it was hard not to feel outnumbered by all the pallets. Sighing, he began to untwist another piece of wire. The sailing was great, but loading and unloading cargo was a total drag.

Cap'n Eli and Greg returned after the next load with good

news—Stanley had found a local builder who'd offered twice what Cap'n Eli had expected for everything they had. The next few bricks seemed a little lighter.

Eliza worked steadily, without any chatter. Each time the dory left, Oliver promised himself he'd ask about her family—their family. But he couldn't figure out a way to start the conversation without coming off all googly-eyed, like Greg. Besides, he'd caught her staring a few times. She must be wondering why he looked so much like her oldest brother. His Uncle Otis.

The cabin bricks went last. When the final load had been transferred to the skiff, Greg climbed up onto Surprise. Cap'n Eli beckoned to Eliza.

"You come ashore this last time, Liza Nell. There's something we need to do."

The skiff headed into shore again, Eliza's back as stiff and straight as the wall someone might build someday with all those cussed bricks.

Squatting down against the cabin, Greg watched her go. "He wants her to call home," he explained. "Doesn't want her dad to worry. She doesn't want to call 'cause she knows he'll be hopping mad. The guy sounds like a tyrant."

"Not really." Oliver sat down on an empty pallet. "He just doesn't understand why she left, right when he needs her most."

"How do you know?"

"Grampa talked about Eliza all the time. He told me once he wouldn't wish that on anyone, a daughter running away."

Waiting for Greg to reach into his pocket, Oliver forced his stiff fingers to uncurl against his thigh.

"Can I—" he stopped. "Can I see your iPod?"

"Sure thing—here."

It was longer and narrower than Oliver expected, silky cool against his palm.

"How d'you turn it on?"

"Press that center button." Greg sat down next to him,

pointing to the middle of a white circle marked with arrows and text. The screen came to life.

"Battery's almost gone, but you probably have enough to watch a movie clip if you want."

Oliver swallowed once. "Show me."

Reaching over, Greg spun his thumb around the white wheel, scrolling down a short list of videos. He hit the center button again.

"Try that one—I think you'll like it." Greg rotated the thing sideways and placed it back in Oliver's hand.

The title was "Women of Art." Oh boy, what had he gotten himself into?

A familiar painting faded in, a girl in a dark dress. That morphed into another painting, of another girl... followed by another, and another. The heads lined up so well he barely noticed the transitions. Some deep stringed instrument—a cello, maybe—played in the background.

"That one!" Greg pointed. "Doesn't she look like Eliza?"

The whole thing was just—beautiful. When a black and white line drawing with "The End" appeared, Oliver couldn't believe more than two minutes had gone by.

Greg flicked down to 'Nicole Concert.' "This is a friend of mine from school—she's pretty good."

A tall girl in a white sparkly dress held a violin. The conductor raised his hands, the orchestra started, and the girl began to play.

"Bach's Violin Concerto in A minor," Greg said. "Surprising how rarely it's played."

"You really know this girl?"

"Yeah. I go to a special music high school, in Manhattan."

"So you play an instrument? As well as she does?"

"Piano. Cello's my favorite, but I'm not as good on that. Nicole and I play duets sometimes, just for fun."

Oliver pulled his eyes away from the screen to stare at Greg.

He'd expected punk, or heavy metal, or something else loud and mean—not this grownup music.

The girl's whole upper body swayed. He could see the tension in the fingers moving up and down the strings. And the sound—wow.

"This thing's amazing."

"The audio's much richer through the headphones, but I figured I'd better keep those hidden." Reaching a thumb toward the scroll wheel, Greg clicked back to the list of videos.

"I'll show you my other favorite—Pablo Casals. The picture's a little grainy, but—oh." The screen went blank. "I guess the battery's finally done."

Oliver handed over the shiny device, already missing its cool fit against his sore palm. Greg slid it into his pocket.

"Now we can watch the sunset instead," he said.

WOODS HOLE DRAWBRIDGE *The first opening bridge across the entrance to Eel Pond operated from 1914 until the '38 Hurricane left it stuck in the "up" position. The replacement lasted almost seventy years. A new bridge opened in 2009.*

17

B Y THE TIME CAP'N ELI and Eliza returned in the empty skiff, the sun had set. The quiet harbor glowed pink under rough-bottomed clouds.

"Climb aboard, Greg! You too, boy." Cap'n Eli said. "We're going into town to celebrate."

They rowed around the jagged-toothed pen at the corner of the harbor, passed close by a large blue ship, and turned into a narrow channel leading to the drawbridge. The rocks just above the high tide mark were littered with random pieces of boats—a barn door rudder and varnished tiller, a triangular floorboard once painted tan, a square of plywood with jagged waterlogged edges.

Right next to a long pier reaching back into the harbor, two varnished masts stuck up out of the water. What looked like a fancy yacht must now be sitting on the bottom.

At the head of the pier stood a restaurant with plywood over its glass doors and a wood sign that read "The Landfall."

"That's where the chowder came from!" Greg pointed to the seaweed-covered front patio. Then he blushed, realizing his mistake. "Ah—is—uh—that where we're going?"

Eli snorted. "It's been a good day, but not that—"

"What's that?" Oliver pointed up at an orange box that had been knocked over.

"Gas pump."

"What a dumb place to put it, right over the water."

"All those sissy yacht powerboats need a place to get fuel." Without changing his stroke, Cap'n Eli checked over his shoulder to center his course through the bridge. A car rumbled overhead just as they passed under the metal grid.

Inside Eel Pond, the shoreline crept away in an almost perfect circle. Two boats were beached, but most swung on moorings in the middle of the pond just like normal. The water sparkled with lights from a wooden building built out over the harbor on pilings.

The aroma of frying fish set his nose quivering. Anything but Johnnycakes would be fine.

Eli rowed them into a dock with a sign that said "Carol can't stop us from pumping your gas." A frayed canvas belt ran from inside another orange gas pump to a winch on the back of a nearby tractor. The whole thing looked totally sketchy.

Cap'n Eli didn't even notice. He raced up a narrow cobblestone alley and turned left so fast that Greg, Eliza and Oliver practically had to run to catch up.

Across the street, a huge stone building topped by a white cupola stood behind a blue sign: "Woods Hole Oceanographic Institution, 1930." The rest of town looked pretty ordinary, all weathered shingles and white trim either side of the drawbridge. The sidewalk still had some seaweedy patches, and a stack of wooden bins stood empty in front of a place called Tsiknas' Food Store.

Just up the street Cap'n Eli took a sharp left into a gloomy doorway, beneath a round sign advertising "Ballantine on Tap."

Eliza followed him inside, and Greg followed Eliza. Oliver hesitated—he'd never been in a bar before, and he was barefoot.

Cap'n Eli stuck his head out the door. "Joining us?"

"Is it okay?"

"You're not one of them anti-liquor types, are ya? I can't abide that. Man's gotta have his–"

"It's not that! It's just—I'm kind of young."

Cap'n Eli laughed. "Come on inside. This place has the best grub in town."

Oliver stepped up into a wood-paneled room and followed Cap'n Eli's black rubber boots along a narrow bar, back into the smoky gloom. Burly men and a few women clustered around tables. The wide boards creaked under his feet, a line of water glistening through the gaps. This must be the lighted place he'd seen hovering out over the inner harbor.

Eliza and Greg had already claimed a round table, and Greg patted the upended barrel right next to him. As soon as Oliver sat down, Greg unwrapped a white cord from his lap and leaned back to plug it into the wall—his charger! Jeez, the guy had nerve.

A large man with a grubby white apron came out from a doorway behind the bar.

"Greetings, Cap'n Eli! Your timin's as good as ever—we just got power back this afternoon. Yesterday and the day before was beer only. Warm beer, at that."

"Good to see you, Jimmy." Cap'n Eli shook the meaty hand before settling onto an upended barrel between Eliza and Oliver. "You must've had plenty of customers in here drownin' their sorrows the last few days."

"Aye, we did. Fella was in last night who owns that nice ketch, the one just off the Landfall? Sunk right there while he was watching, no insurance. After a few drinks, he swore he'd raise her somehow." Jimmy swiped a rag across the wood tabletop. "And a course all the loonies from Hadley's practically slept here, since their private ferry stopped running."

Table clean, he stuck the rag in his belt.

"So what brings you back to Woods Hole?"

"Load of bricks from New Bedford—and some godawful noisy chickens. Sold everything on the spot, so I told the crew we'd celebrate."

"All these folks?" Jimmy's gaze went around the table. "You must be makin' good money again."

"Special occasion," Cap'n Eli replied. "In fact Greg's getting off here in–"

A squeak from Greg was cut off by Oliver's kick under the table. Something tumbled onto the floor—something shiny. Oliver didn't dare look down.

"So whatcha got to eat?" Cap'n Eli was asking. "We're all powerful hungry from slingin' bricks all day."

"How 'bout lobster? Two for one tonight, hurricane special. When the power went off, Hank at the fish market put all the lobsters in his fridge truck and started it up—ran for two days straight. Cussed diesel was so loud I went down there this morning and told him I'd buy the rest, just to get some quiet."

Eli nodded once. "Then lobster it is. And I'll take my usual— pint of Narragansett. Give these kids whatever they want."

"Root beer, please." Eliza spoke first.

"Same here," Greg said. His left thumb and forefinger had inched the white cord up his leg until the wide plug at the end appeared—with nothing attached. So the MP3 player was still down there somewhere, underneath the table.

Oliver looked up to find Jimmy staring at him.

"D'you have, uh—ginger ale?"

"Course we do! Take a Martian invasion to run us out of that."

If Jimmy could see down through the table, he might wonder if the Martians had invaded after all.

RUM *The word probably originates from "rumbullion," a tumult or uproar. Also British slang for "the best," as in "having a rum time."*

18

"PSST, OLIVER," GREG WHISPERED, once Jimmy had gone back to the bar. "You gotta look— it must've landed over near you." He slid the charger back into his pocket.

Oliver dragged the floor with his left foot. He located the table base, the edge of his barrel seat, and Cap'n Eli's right boot ("Whatcha doin', boy?"). He shook his head once to let Greg know there was nothing else. Maybe the player had slid down through one of the gaps in the floor—it was thin enough.

Their drinks arrived, and after one toast to Surprise and another to the crew, Cap'n Eli downed his beer and ordered another. He was halfway through his second when Stanley dragged up a barrel and sat down between Oliver and Cap'n Eli. Still in khaki.

That's why he looked familiar—Stanley was the khaki guy! With black hair, a potbelly, and that shiny clean-shaven chin, Oliver hadn't recognized him.

"Can I sell you a lobster, Stanley?" Jimmy asked. "Half price."

Stanley shook his head. "Seen enough of those damn things coming up in my nets. Just the usual, thanks."

"Charlie!" Jimmy shouted to the bartender. "We got any of that dark rum left? If so I need a double, on the—" Jimmy turned back to Stanley. "Sorry, no ice till tomorrow."

Stanley shrugged. "Liver won't know the difference."

A dimpled glass of dark brown liquid arrived and Stanley downed it in one swallow. "Ahh. That was so good, I think I'll have another."

"And it's on me tonight," Eli said, clinking his empty mug against the rim of Stanley's glass. "Thanks for your help today."

"Nice to get something done." Stanley sighed. "Boatyard phone just rings and rings, since the storm."

Oliver hadn't had lobster since his tenth birthday, when Grampa bartered some engine repair for a dozen shedders. Everyone had eaten two that night. This time he filled up on the French fries and canned green beans.

Eliza cracked open each claw with her bare hands. Between bites, Greg admired her. He didn't seem too worried about his missing electronics.

Meanwhile Stanley, who had matched Cap'n Eli drink for drink, began to slur his words. Raising an arm to call for another, he capsized the barrel he was sitting on and landed hard. He crawled back to his feet, giggling, and righted his seat. But instead of sitting down again he picked something up off the floor.

"Whassis?" He held up a thin sliver of silver.

"That's mine—must've fallen out of my pocket." Greg reached for it, but Stanley pulled away.

"Didn't ask whose-is-it, asked what-is-it." One thumb settled onto the scroll wheel as he tried to focus on the tiny screen. "Looks like something a Martian'd carry. So where's your shiny space suit?"

Eli chuckled. Eliza's laugh tinkled. Oliver joined in, nervously. If the thing came on...

Greg's long fingers drummed the table.

"Sir, I just—"

"He's got that fancy wristwatch, too," Cap'n Eli added, winking at Oliver. "Maybe he's a Russian spy."

"Thassit!" Stanley smacked his empty palm against the table. "Remember that big bomb a few years ago? I saw a picture of the thing that set it off, about this size. Blew up an entire city."

Fresh drinks arrived, and empty glasses disappeared. Stanley sat down again, still studying the blank screen.

"Really, sir. It's not for setting off bombs." Greg held out his hand again. "It's just—" he stopped.

Just what? *Just* held more music than the bar's jukebox? Or *just* played movies in color, with a better picture than the local theater? Oliver's stomach lurched—there was nothing Greg could say.

Stanley shook it twice, held it up to his ear, and turned it over to squint at the tiny writing on the back. "Well, I don't know what the hell it is, or where it came from." He rocked back on his stool. "But I was in the bomb squad during the war, so I know how to fix it."

Before Oliver could stop him, Stanley raised his hand and dropped the shiny device directly into his fresh drink. Rum splashed brown onto Oliver's arm. Then with the player pinched against the rim, Stanley drained the glass in one long swallow and thunked it down again, smiling.

"Ah, she makes a fine mixer."

Cap'n Eli and Stanley laughed. And laughed, and laughed some more. Cap'n Eli had to wipe away the tears running down his cheeks. Greg's eyes remained frozen on his rum-soaked player. And Eliza's left eyebrow raised into that perfect vee, like she was wondering—what IS that, anyway?

Oliver could only be sure of one thing—an iPod on the rocks was way better than a suspected Martian behind bars.

PAINTER *A line attached to the bow of a small boat, used to tie it to a dock or another vessel.*

19

FOUR DRINKS LATER, THE ROOM had gotten too loud to hear. When Stanley's head dropped to the table, Cap'n Eli paid the bill and stood up.

"Time to go." He helped Stanley to his feet and pointed him toward the door. Halfway there, a burly fisherman offered up a stool and Stanley lurched down onto it, waving goodbye.

Cap'n Eli followed Greg and Eliza back out into the street. Greg casually dropped his arm around Eliza's waist, and she didn't pull away.

"I can row if you want, sir," Oliver said, to distract himself.

"I'll be fine, now I'm out in the fresh air." Hiccupping, Cap'n Eli stumbled off the curb and back up onto it again. "That's why I stay away from rum. Stanley won't be good for much tomorrow."

"And where do we go, tomorrow?"

"That'll sort itself out. I keep thinkin' each cargo will be our last, and then another appears. Just got to keep going."

"Yes, sir." Oliver swallowed hard. "Do you think we could go back to Hadley's?"

"I thought you young bucks would prefer the big city of Woods Hole. Hahaha!" He let his head fall back so his laughter rose straight to the stars.

"Well, it's just that…"

"Spit it out, boy," Cap'n Eli growled.

"I overheard Greg say he'd come from a different time. I think he said the next century or something crazy."

"Kid's gonna end up in the loony bin."

"But didn't Jimmy say the people who live on Naushon are loonies? Maybe we need to bring Greg back where he came from."

"Jimmy was just grousing." Cap'n Eli's gaze landed on the double shadow just ahead. "But we gotta do something. I sure can't be feedin' him forever, not the way he eats."

Back aboard Surprise, Cap'n Eli stumbled right into his bunk. Eliza disappeared below too. Oliver wrapped the skiff's painter around the stern cleat, wondering if it would be all right for him to crawl into his bunk too—he could barely keep his eyes open.

"Psst—up here." Greg waved him forward to where bricks and chickens had been stacked high that morning. Now there was nothing between cabin and mainmast but red dust and a tumble of empty pallets.

"What did you say to him?" Greg whispered. "I rushed out 'cause I thought he was going to leave me behind."

"I told him you're crazy, which wasn't hard for him to believe. He's gonna take us back to Hadley's."

"And how do we get from there back to—"

A rumbling snore rose up through the companionway. Greg snickered.

"I don't know yet," Oliver replied. "But at least we'd be in the right place for something to happen." He looked up toward the sky. "Do the stars here look different?"

"I wouldn't know—you can't see them at all, in the city."

"Especially when your eyes are focused down on a tiny screen." Oliver shook his head. "I thought they were gonna lock you up."

"Me too. I'd forgotten all about that stupid thing until Stanley picked it off the floor." He stretched the fingers of his left hand back so far they almost touched his bony wrist. "It's so strange—I'm never bored here like I am at home. Everything we do seems to make a difference. You get up in the middle of the night to deliver bricks, and when you arrive everyone's waiting to see what you've got."

"Same stuff happens at home, you know."

"But here I can keep track of everything! There's so much going on at home—I feel like I need a rewind button."

A foghorn wailed, somewhere over near the ferry dock.

"Hey, if we ever get home again?" Greg picked a loose chip of paint off the corner of the cabin top. "Maybe you and I can go sailing on Surprise again."

"Without your mom?"

Greg snorted. "That's way too much to hope for." He dropped a narrow hand onto Oliver's shoulder. "I'm glad you came with me, Oliver. You really fit in—and Cap'n Eli respects the hell out of you."

"But I didn't come with you." Oliver grinned up at him. "You came with ME."

COASTERS *By the mid-twentieth century, coasting schooners had been replaced by trucks for most long distance cargo transport. Schooners continued to make local deliveries, especially across bays or between islands.*

20

JUST AFTER DAWN, THE FRYING pan crashed off the stove again. Maybe this time he could figure out why.

Oliver followed the twine up the companionway, aft along the cockpit, and back to the transom where it turned down into the water and disappeared. Gingerly pulling it in, he found a small weight tied the end.

"Soon as Surprise turns with a change in the tide, that weight pulls the pan off the stove." Cap'n Eli had come on deck too and now he took the lead piece from Oliver, swinging it like a pendulum. "First captain I ever sailed with showed me this trick. Damn sight more reliable than a ship's clock that stops every time you fall off a wave."

Swinging a leg over the transom into the skiff, Cap'n Eli winked. "And the early bird catches the cargo, you know."

But just after noon, he rowed back out to Surprise with short, grumpy strokes.

"Only one thing needs moving today, and that's trash. I'd run Surprise up on Grassy Island before I'd use her as a garbage scow."

That afternoon, Greg caught a fat cod. After filleting it he carefully saved the skeleton for Eliza to make chowder. She fried up the cheeks, and Oliver had to agree with Cap'n Eli— they were nothing special.

Once his plate was empty, Greg turned to Oliver with a surprising question. "Will you teach me to row?"

"Great idea," Cap'n Eli said. "Just stay close to shore, and watch the current. You'll end up in Hadley's if you get sucked out into the Hole."

"We'll be careful," Oliver promised.

He settled onto the stern thwart of the skiff. Greg sat down in the middle, between the two oars.

"You'll have to untie us first."

"Oh!" Standing, Greg unwrapped the painter from the cleat and dropped it in the bow of the skiff. "Now what?"

"Oars go in between those—I think they're called tholes." Oliver pointed to the wooden dowels sticking up from the rail. "Put the outboard one in first, then push away from Surprise and drop the other in. Don't let go or they'll fall overboard. Ready? Pull with both arms at the same time."

Greg's long fingers wrapped around the fat handles so far that their tips touched his palms. Tongue tucked into the right corner of his mouth, he began to row.

His right arm was better coordinated, so he circled to starboard.

"Both arms have to pull the same amount, at the same time," Oliver said. "I'll count off, okay? Stroke. Stroke. Stroke…"

After five or six pulls, Greg's course steadied into a straight line. Right toward the Yacht Club's stone pier.

"Now turn to starboard. Or port, or—stop!"

The bow crunched against the seaweedy rocks. Fortunately they'd been going really slow.

"Why didn't you tell me I was gonna hit something?" The oars dangled helplessly from Greg's hands.

"I tried." Oliver sighed. "Push off with the near oar—harder. Okay, now just row with the starboard one—your left hand. Turn us around. That's it—"

The skiff began a slow pirouette. Once they were parallel to the beach, Greg began to pull with both arms again.

"Longer strokes," Oliver suggested. "Brace your feet so you can use your back and leg muscles."

This skiff reminded him of Sparky, his boat at home. Same u-shaped stern thwart, same thin floorboards that flexed just a little underfoot. Maybe they'd been built at the same time?

While Greg found his groove, Oliver checked out the shoreline cleanup. Rollers and long boards had been set in place to slide boats back down to the water on the next high tide. Up near the head of the harbor, two men stood on the bottom of a large blue ketch, refastening her sprung planks.

Above the beach, shingled houses blacked out the setting sun. Windows blinked, reflecting the water's glint like large friendly eyes.

One lonely sailboat swung to her mooring. An arc of gold leaf spelled out "Josephine."

"That's the boat Stanley was going on about," Oliver said. "Her captain ran the motor during the storm to take some of the strain off the mooring, but it got too hot and caught fire."

Greg was concentrating so hard he didn't reply. His even strokes left deep eddies in the water on either side of the skiff.

"Your mom'd be proud," Oliver said softly.

Greg snorted. "Easy to learn stuff when she's not trying to jam it down my throat." The tip of his sunburnt nose was starting to peel.

They circled the edge of the harbor until the bow pointed back toward Surprise. The beach stepped up into a rock wall, and the wall turned a corner where a white flagpole stood guard. Perfect grass rolled up to a house still glowing in the last bit of sun.

Around the corner was a channel leading out to the Hole. The water under them began to spill downstream, tugging at the skiff, as if the large center rockpile was reeling them in.

"Head a little more to port, into the harbor," Oliver suggested. "Otherwise we'll get sucked into—Jeez, what're you doing?"

Greg had stopped rowing.

"We could let the current take us back to Hadley's," Greg said softly. "Waiting for Cap'n Eli might—"

"That won't work! We need to be on Surprise."

"How do you know?"

"I just—know. Anyway, I'm not going to steal Cap'n Eli's skiff after everything he's done for us. We'll get—"

"Everything he's—we're like indentured servants! Especially Eliza. He treats her like—"

"Like a first mate." Gripping the wooden thwart either side of his thighs, Oliver shook his head. "We all work hard, together. That's different than slaving away for a lazy boss."

Surprise disappeared behind the shrub-covered island on the far side of the channel.

"He'll take us back to Hadley's," Oliver promised. "We just have to be patient."

"What happens next, in the log?"

"I've been trying to remember. I didn't pay much attention to specific dates."

"So you don't know if he goes back to Hadley's again."

"For sure he goes back—I'm just not sure exactly when."

"We've already been here four days, you know. And my school starts next week."

"I know. But we've gotta stay with Surprise—she's the key."

A flash caught his eye, down beneath the surface. Shiny ribbons of seaweed streamed down-current, combed by the water rushing and swirling out through the narrowing channel. The current would be even stronger when they got to the narrow part ahead—too strong to row against.

The watery dance below was almost hypnotizing. He forced himself to look up again.

"Come on, Greg."

Heaving a sigh, Greg tugged on the starboard oar to turn the bow around. He began to row again, his just-learned strokes grabbing neat pockets of water on either side of the skiff.

They weren't making any headway.

"Pull harder," Oliver directed. "The current's winning."

The two blades dug in deep, and Greg's biceps strained and bulged. He crabbed one stroke, grabbing more air than water—and they lost distance again, sucked toward the white tumbling water of the Hole.

"I can't–" Greg's forehead glistened, a sudden wrinkled roadmap of panic.

"Move over—we'll both row."

Sliding onto the seat next to Greg, Oliver took hold of the port oar.

"Ready? Stroke! Stroke…"

He pulled as hard and as rhythmically as he could, focusing only on the blade's sharp entry into the water and the gurgle as he pulled it out again. Hardening blisters chafed against the wooden handles.

Greg matched his efforts, their wobbly course fetching up straight after the first few strokes.

A glance over his shoulder told Oliver they were gaining on the flagpole—just.

"Stroke, stroke…"

Sweat had glued the T-shirt to his back by the time they reached the harbor and Surprise reappeared behind the island. Oliver slid back to the aft thwart, gasping for breath. The only other sound across the darkening water was the rhythmic gurgle of Greg's even strokes, pulling for Surprise.

BLUEFISH *A strongly flavored fish common to the summer waters around Cape Cod.*

21

J UST BEFORE NOON THE NEXT day, Cap'n Eli rowed his grumpy strokes back out to Surprise. Eliza grabbed the painter from him.

"Time to move on, sir?"

"Past time." Cap'n Eli rubbed a hand across his face. "We'll head back to New Bedford, see if there's anything there."

Fortunately Greg was down below and didn't hear.

Cap'n Eli raised one hand to shade his eyes against the midday glare. Oliver followed his gaze across the calm harbor, out to where the small buoys dipped and bobbed under the rushing current.

"But we won't get through the Hole until the wind picks up or the current slacks off. Which gives us time to bust some rust."

"Crikey!" Eliza groaned. "That's the worst job in the world."

"Yup. I always save it for when I'm really mad about

something. When it's done, life don't seem so bad. Here you go—" reaching into the lazarette, Cap'n Eli handed her a short brush with bronze bristles. "Start with the windlass and work aft, and don't forget the cowl vent behind the foremast. I'll follow along and touch up the bare spots."

"And me?" Oliver piped up.

"Here, take this." Cap'n Eli handed Oliver a stubby broom. "Clean up all that brick dust."

"I did that yesterday—"

"Well, do it again!"

"What should I do?" Greg's shaggy head appeared in the companionway.

"Jaysus, all these people to keep busy! You can clean up the cabin. And try to get the dirt into the trash bin this time."

Oliver swept his way forward, collecting the paint chips from the windlass last. Once he had a dustpan full of white, he started aft.

Eliza glanced up. "Just dump it overboard."

"I can't do that!"

Eliza snorted. "Even if you put it in the trash, it'll eventually go out on the garbage scow and get dumped over the side somewhere else. Might as well save someone all that extra work."

"Is that really what happens?"

"What'd you think?" She gave him a funny look before turning her brush to the hood that let air into the cargo hold.

Oliver couldn't bring himself to dump paint chips into the harbor, so he carried the dustpan below and tipped it into the trash. Greg was just putting the soft broom away in its narrow locker.

"You gotta stop him!" Greg grabbed Oliver's sleeve. "I heard him say he's heading back to New Bedford. We might never get home!"

"Shh, calm down. We go right past Hadley's."

"But he might not stop!" Greg squeaked.

Putting a finger to his lips, Oliver climbed back up on deck.

By the time Cap'n Eli had covered all the bare metal with a thick smelly paint, the seabreeze had filled and the current had turned. Greg and Oliver pulled up the main while Eliza upped anchor—hopefully avoiding the wet paint spots on the windlass. Mainsail filling on starboard tack, Cap'n Eli called for the jumbo.

Once they could clear Grassy Island's red and white beacon, Eli tacked onto port for the reach through the Hole. Oliver stood near the wheel, itching to steer. He could sail them through—and maybe just somehow end up in Hadley's? The entrance buoys were already visible against the green land.

Cap'n Eli sniffed the breeze, so Oliver did too. Salt water, sun-beaten grass, the toe-curling smell of bird poop—and something damp, like rotting wood.

"More weather coming," Cap'n Eli muttered. "Rain, anyway."

Hazy blue sky arched from east to west.

"Hadley Harbor might be just the spot for tonight." A blue-eyed wink, so quick Oliver almost missed it.

He hadn't forgotten!

"Hey—I got a fish!" Greg ran aft to the line stretching taut off the transom.

"Well, haul it in before someone else has it for dinner."

This one was a real tail-thumper. Greg had two dark fillets ready for Eliza's pan before they reached the Hadley's beacon, and he caught Oliver's eye to share a smile as they sailed in between the small entrance buoys.

The islands rose up, welcoming Surprise back again. Nonomessett, Uncatena, Naushon—each sandy cliff and green scrub hill looked as untouched as it would fifty years later.

Eli kept sailing at full speed, even though they were closing fast with the backside of little Bull Island.

Twenty yards. Ten, then five…

"Hard-a-lee!" Eli spun the wheel to port. Surprise passed through head to wind, sails shuddering, and fell off onto starboard tack. Now her bow was pointing right at the enormous tan gargoyle of rock on the port side of the entrance, only a few lengths away.

They ran out of room before they were back up to full speed.

"Hard-a-lee!" Surprise made a more sluggish turn, the tip of her bowsprit crossing over the gargoyle's head.

Now what? They were headed for the starboard side of the entrance, with not enough speed or room to tack again. Oliver grabbed onto the lifeline, bracing for the crunch—and instead heard the luffing of sails. Cap'n Eli couldn't be tacking—Surprise was barely moving. And he hadn't said anything–

Just before the bow came through the wind, Cap'n Eli straightened out the wheel. They ghosted past the rocks on momentum, sails fluttering. The gargoyle slid by a few feet to leeward.

They were in!

With the rocks astern Cap'n Eli bore away, wind pressing silence back into the canvas overhead. So that's how it was done, without an engine.

Hadley's felt like home. The dayboats had been bailed and lined up ready to sail again. Sailboats swung on moorings in the inner harbor—he recognized the blue hull of Mariah. And the only sign of the beached Starlight was the huge dent left behind by her keel.

"Lower jumbo."

Liza pulled down the sail, and Greg helped her furl it against the boom. Oliver strode forward to the main halyards.

"Lower main."

Cap'n Eli spun the wheel and Surprise turned into the wind again, losing speed as she closed with the far shore.

"Drop anchor."

Surprise clanked back against her chain.

Glancing around, Oliver had to swallow a grin. They'd ended up in almost exactly the same spot where Surprise would christen her new anchor, fifty years from now.

Clouds had filled in along the southern horizon and now they dashed across the setting sun, throwing strange shadows onto the deck. Cap'n Eli stood near the stern, sniffing the air again.

"We've got another blow coming—a big one."

"Can't be! I don't..." Oliver stopped.

"Oh it's not unusual, two big storms only a few days apart— it's almost like the first one clears a path." He rubbed his face. "I'm gonna trust my nose this time and put out that mother of a second anchor."

"I'll help." Oliver scrambled to his feet.

By the time they loaded the awkward anchor into the skiff, rowed it out to the northwest, and cleated the still soggy line, Eliza had served up dinner.

"Eating on deck again?" Cap'n Eli asked. "You'll never turn me into a sissy yachtie, you know."

"It's too stuffy in the cabin, even with the skylight open. And it reeks of kerosene."

"That's because I refilled the stove this morning. All your fancy cooking burned a whole tank of valuable fuel."

After a few hearty bites, Cap'n Eli glanced across the cockpit at Greg, who hadn't touched his food. "Dontcha like bluefish?"

Greg shrugged. "It's just that it was so beautifully alive, only a few hours ago."

"So was the cod you gobbled up last night."

"Cod doesn't have quite so much—spirit. This fish fought back hard."

"Ayuh—blues don't die easy. But we've gotta eat something to stay alive, and a steady diet of one thing gets right boring." Cap'n Eli lowered his bushy eyebrows. "You're a funny one, Castaway Greg."

After finishing his own meal, Cap'n Eli grabbed Greg's piece and shoveled that down too. Then he sat back with a satisfied belch, eyes moving around the harbor and up each piece of rigging.

Oliver listened to the wind whistling aloft, his stomach lurching—tonight must be the night. So would they get sick again? Maybe that's why Greg hadn't eaten his dinner. He hadn't seemed very worried about the fish's spirit when he stuck a knife in its belly.

After handing the dirty dishes down the companionway, Oliver pushed past Greg and climbed below.

"Liza?" He lifted the drying towel off its hook next to the stove. "Ah—how's your Pa doing?"

"I really don't know. I tried to call, that day we offloaded all those bricks, but he didn't answer. He hates the phone." Her hands moved quickly, swiping the dishes with a rag and then rinsing them with hot water from the kettle. Mom's hands, without the age spots.

Her T-shirt smelled of sweat and mothballs.

"What'd your mom die of?"

"Lots of questions tonight, boy."

He dried the first plate, picked up the next. And then, so softly he almost missed it, she answered.

"Something was wrong with her insides. She was sick for so long, it was almost a relief when she finally passed."

"I'm sorry."

"She knew I was itching to get out, but she never once asked me to stay. I left four brothers and a baby sister at home." Eliza pressed the knuckles of a soapy hand against her forehead. "I don't know how my Pa's going to cope."

"He'll cope fine," Oliver predicted. "He always does."

Eliza turned to stare down at him. "You know Pa?"

Uh. "Cap'n Eli talks about him a lot."

"Of course—they're best friends." She sniffled once. "Pa just assumed I'd take over the housework—I had to get out before he got used to that. I don't mind doing dishes as part of my job. But I hate it on shore where it's expected, just 'cause I'm the only girl."

"So you'll never go back?"

"Oh I don't know. I'd like to. Someday." Handing Oliver the last dish, she wiped her hands on the cotton towel he'd been using. "I want to see a bit of the world first, you know? Not just marry Jerry Long and settle down."

Vince Long's dad? She was supposed to marry the local mechanic?

"Now he'll probably marry Jeannie Sykes."

Vince's mother's name was Jeannie—and Oliver'd heard

his parents were getting a divorce.

"Won't you miss it? Home I mean?"

"If I do I know how to get back." She smiled, her cheeks crinkling. "Thanks, it helps to talk about it. And now it's time to turn in. Cap'n Eli's got a good nose for weather, so it could be a rough night."

HURRICANE LIGHTNING *Although rare, hurricanes do sometimes produce lightning. Usually the energy is translated into high winds instead.*

22

A LAST HINT OF BLOOD-ORANGE SKY had just faded to black when the wind began to moan. The long sunset had been awesome, racing clouds tossing their colors down onto the water—first gold, then orange, then purple-black. Now Surprise began to lurch sideways, tacking back and forth as the wind tried to free her from her anchor chain.

Creeping down the companionway ladder, Oliver poked at the lump in Greg's bunk.

"Wake up," he whispered. "It's time."

No answer, except a rumbling snore from Eli's bunk.

Oliver poked harder, finally pulling back the blanket—to find a lumpy pillow, carefully staged to look like a person lying on his side.

The bunk just aft of Greg's was empty too. *"Time to turn in,"* Eliza'd said. Yeah, right.

Oliver scrambled back up the companionway, stumbling

against the coaming as Surprise leaned over sideways in a sharp wind gust. In the next lull, he heard whispering in the bow.

"Psst, Greg!"

A stubby silence, then Eliza's voice rose into a question mark. After a quick reply Greg shuffled aft, alone.

Oliver tugged his sleeve back toward the cockpit. "We have to go—"

"So go." Greg pulled out of Oliver's grip. "I'm staying here, with Liza."

Was he kidding? It was so dark Oliver couldn't read his face. "You can't do that!"

"You told me she ran away to sea and never came back. So I'll just run away with her."

"It's not that simple." Oliver sighed. "The tiniest little thing can affect the future. We've probably already screwed things up just being here a few days. Who knows what'd happen if you stayed?"

"Who knows what would happen if I went back?" Greg bit at a hangnail, just like he used to when Oliver first knew him. "Life goes too fast for me, in our time."

"You don't have to get so caught up in everything."

"I know I don't. But I just—do." Greg stuffed his hands into pockets. "I like who I am here a lot better."

Oliver liked this Greg better too. But—

"You have to come back with me," he repeated. "What about your music, and that girl Nicole? And what would I tell your Mom?"

"I didn't eat any of that bluefish, you know. I'm not gonna get sick again, just to go home."

"I don't think that's it—I feel fine." Oliver pointed overhead. "Don't you hear the wind? There's another storm coming tonight."

The whistle in the rigging had climbed several notes up the scale. Hard to believe Surprise would survive another big blow and live another fifty years—all so she could be rebuilt into what Cap'n Eli would call a "sissy yacht."

"I'd like to stay too," Oliver admitted. "I love sailing cargoes around, even though it's a lot more work than I thought."

"We could both stay."

Oliver shook his head. "No way—we're going back, together."

After a quick glance forward, Greg scraped long fingers against a bristly cheek. "How?"

"We sit in the cockpit and look at the clouds, the sails, the water—anything that's the same in both times. If that doesn't work..." Oliver shrugged. "I guess we try again tomorrow night."

"Not much of a plan."

"Got a better idea?"

"No." Greg heaved a sigh. "Just let me–"

"Don't say goodbye," Oliver reminded him.

Greg shuffled back to the bow.

Oliver crept aft and sat down on the cockpit seat. Pulling his knees up into his chest, he listened forward. All he could hear was the wind.

A thick bolt of gold lightning slashed a jagged seam in the sky. Hurricanes didn't make lightning, did they?

And how long was it gonna take for Greg to say one lousy goodbye?

When he couldn't stand it any longer, Oliver marched all the way forward. A two-headed shadow leaned against the foremast.

"Greg!" he hissed.

A hand waved him away.

"We've gotta go—now!"

Greg crawled to his feet and dragged Oliver aft, out of earshot. "I was just about to tell her," he whispered. "It's not an easy thing to explain." A cloud of mist swirled around his shoulders.

"I told you, you can't–"

"But I can't just leave."

"Yes you can."

"No, I can't." Greg's eyes dropped. "That's what my dad did, and it hurts too much."

A second bolt of lightning struck a pine tree just off the bow, so close Oliver could smell the after-sizzle of burnt needles.

"Then you'd better get it over with," Oliver said. "This storm's moving really fast, and–"

"What are you two whispering about?" Eliza had followed Greg aft.

"Um, Oliver was just explaining why lightning–"

"Stop stalling," Oliver interrupted. "I'll tell her the truth."

"But you said we–"

Oliver held up his hand. "It's the only way."

Eliza's dark eyes glinted, so familiar—but without Mom's framework of crinkly lines.

"I'm your nephew," he told her. "The son of your baby sister Josie."

"That can't be—she's only three months old!"

Oliver inhaled as much air as he could, to support his words. "We're from the future, the next century. And tonight's our best chance to get home. That's why Greg has to leave."

"Crikey!" Her eyes narrowed. "That would explain why you look so much like Otis. But how did you–"

"We don't have time to explain. And it doesn't make much sense anyway. You'll just have to believe me."

"Why should I?"

"Because my name is—Jeez!" Another crackle and flash lit up the whole harbor. "That was close."

Eliza's dark eyes had focused to slits. "Tell me your name."

"Oliver."

"After my pa?" Eliza gasped.

Oliver nodded, a lump in his throat. "He was–" he stopped. She wouldn't want to know Grampa was gone. And telling her only made it more true.

"He's gonna be okay," Oliver said finally. "Even without you."

Face crumpling, Eliza pushed fists against her eyelids.

"Shoot, Oliver!" Greg's dark eyes were huge. "You said it would change the future if we told anyone!"

Oliver kept his gaze on Eliza. "You won't tell anyone else, will you, Liza? Especially not Cap'n Eli?"

She shook her head, face still hidden behind dampening fingers.

"Good. Now come on—we've gotta go." Oliver pulled on Greg's sleeve.

"Adieu, Sweet Liza." Greg reached out to push back a lock of her hair, his hand lingering.

"Jeez, Greg—come on."

Dragging him aft with one hand, Oliver waved goodbye with the other. "Maybe we'll meet again, someday..."

SPAR *Any of the long poles (mast, boom, gaff) that support sails. Aluminum replaced wood as the standard building material in the middle of the twentieth century.*

23

GREG COLLAPSED ON THE COCKPIT seat across from Oliver. "What makes you so sure looking at a bunch of stupid waves is gonna get us home again?"

Oliver wasn't sure at all—he wasn't even sure he wanted this to work. He felt so at home here in the past. Maybe this was his last chance to stay where he belonged?

Thick damp air swirled between their faces, as wet as mist could be without actually raining. Every single one of Oliver's arm hairs stood up with the moisture, like tiny hands voting. But what were they voting for—stay or go?

He was just stalling, he knew.

"All we can do is try," he told Greg.

He let his head fall back, eyes climbing the shadow of Surprise's towering mainmast. Eliza's tear-stained face kept swimming into his mind. Was it wrong to tell her? Seemed like the only way to get Greg away. And this storm tonight was for sure their best chance, with all the electricity in the air. If he could only concentrate—

Another bolt hit, over Woods Hole.

"Are we gonna get struck by lightning?" Greg squeaked.

"It's pretty far away."

He tried to empty his mind, like going to sleep.

Which was completely impossible, with Greg staring at him.

"Let's face aft," Oliver suggested.

Greg swung his long legs up onto the cockpit seat, wrapping elbows around his knees to mirror Oliver. The black jeans were almost white now, from all the salt spray.

"What am I supposed to be thinking about?" he asked.

"Don't think," Oliver replied. "What's your happiest memory?"

"When I first saw Eliza on the—"

"No! Something at home."

"The only thing that makes me happy at home is my cello. And virtual reality games."

"So—imagine you're inside your favorite game. Or just concentrate on your breathing."

"My breathing? What's that got to do with—"

"Will you just shut up and TRY?"

Closing his eyes, Oliver let his body be swayed by the motion of Surprise. Sounds swirled around him—the moan of wind, a loose halyard swatting one of the masts nearby, harbor waves lapping against the length of his favorite schooner.

He was really zoning out, had almost forgotten where he was—when Greg swiveled back to face him.

"It's not working."

"Jeez, Greg, give it some time!" Another bolt of lightning landed in the trees, yellow-white and spookily silent.

The mist had finally turned to raindrops—he could hear them pinging the deck. And that slapping halyard had gotten even louder—tinnier, too, as if it were banging against metal instead of wood.

"I was almost there," Oliver said.

"How d'you know—where's there?"

"I just kinda forgot where I was. That's gotta be good for time travel, don't you think?"

Greg stood up. "This is never going to work. I'm gonna go check on Liza. We shouldn't have left her up there–"

"Honey! Where's your rain jacket? You'll catch your death again."

Mrs H? What was–

"Mom!"

Greg reached up for a hug—until he remembered himself. Raising his arms overhead into a stretch instead, he sat down again. "I was just—Oliver was teaching me about the stars."

"But it's pouring! And you can't see anything under the awning."

"That's exactly what I told him. I'm going to bed." Pushing past his mother, Greg disappeared below.

"Oliver?" Another woman spoke, low and throaty. "You coming down too?"

For just a moment Oliver wondered if he'd stayed behind, with Eliza—this voice reminded him so much of the one he'd last heard asking his name.

"Mom."

She came up into the cockpit and sat down next to him, drawing him into the circle of her left arm. He breathed in her familiar scent, a mix of wood shavings and warm cookies— which always seemed so odd since she didn't bake.

"I'm glad you're here," he told her now, the words muffling into her sweatshirt.

"I could hardly stay away once Buck called. I'm glad you're finally feeling up to being on deck again—the last couple days were pretty rough."

"I'll never eat Manhattan chowder again."

"Fine with me." Her arm tightened around his shoulders.

"Mom?"

"Yes, Oliver." Her voice echoed, deep inside her.

"D'you ever hear from Aunt Eliza?"

Pulling away to look at him, her left eyebrow cocked up into a vee.

"I actually got a letter from her, just after you left on Surprise. Why?"

"Where is she?" His neck was cramping, but he wasn't going to move until he absolutely had to.

"Argentina. She's signed on as mate on a yacht going around Cape Horn. Almost seventy, and she won't come ashore! Crazy Aunt Eliza." He felt her head shake back and forth.

Wiping a few drops of rain off her right cheek, Mom tucked her arm in tight around his waist. "She was reminiscing about a storm she lived through, right here on Surprise."

"Hurricane Carol?"

"Hurricane Edna—one week later. Your grampa called it the milk storm, because he couldn't get enough to feed me. It was only a few days after Grandma Nellie died and Eliza ran off— she was working for Cap'n Eli, but Pa didn't know that then."

"She didn't try to call home or anything?"

"Oh I don't know—it was such a long time ago. All Grampa ever talked about was feeding me every four hours. I guess I had a big appetite."

Shivering, Oliver burrowed deeper into his mother's side. "What else did she say? In the letter, I mean."

"Who, Eliza? At the very end she wrote, 'PS, say hi to Oliver.' I can't believe she even remembered your name—she's never met you. And now you ask about her! Strange."

A warm glow spread through him, like an internal blush. "That's because, ah—oh yeah! Mrs. H was reading Cap'n Eli's log the other night. About when Eliza sailed with him."

"Way back when I was just a tiny baby."

"Uh huh. And somehow it seems like, well—yesterday."

Pulling away from the warmth of her sweatshirt, Oliver studied the familiar white laugh lines etched around her eyes.

"Mom, when we get home—can I get an iPod?"

Author's Note

I would like to tell you that every single historical detail of this story is accurate, but there is at least one exception. The Woods Hole town dock was not destroyed by Hurricane Carol, except in my imagination.

FOR MORE INFORMATION

please visit

www.carolnewmancronin.com

GLOSSARY

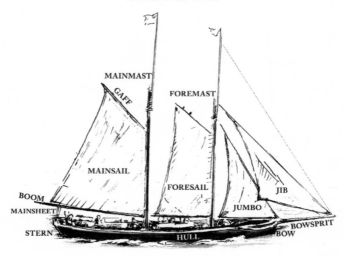

AFT	Toward the stern of a vessel.
BAROMETER	An instrument that measures atmospheric pressure, used at sea to forecast the weather. Also called "the glass."
BEAUFORT SCALE	A method for describing wind speed, based mainly on observed sea conditions.
BELAYING PIN	A metal or wooden pin used to secure a line fastened around it.
BOOM	A long spar used to control the bottom edge of a sail.
BOW	The forward part of a boat.
BOWLINE	A knot used to make a secure loop which is easy to untie, even after it's pulled on hard.
BULKHEAD	A partition separating a boat into cabins that also adds structure to the hull.
CABIN SOLE	The collection of floorboards used to cover the deep interior or bilge in the living spaces of a boat.

CLEAT	A fitting with two projecting horns around which a line may be secured.
COAMING	A raised frame around a hatch or deck area designed to keep water out.
COASTER	A ship sailing along a coast, usually engaged in trade.
COCKPIT	An enclosed area from which a boat is steered, which serves as a gathering place while in harbor.
COMPANIONWAY	An opening that provides access between deck and cabin, usually protected with a sliding hatch.
CURRENT	The horizontal movement of water, usually related to the rise and fall of the tide.
FOREDECK	The forward part of a ship's main deck.
FORESAIL	A square sail set on the foremast, the next mast forward of the mainmast.
GAFF	A spar that supports the top edge of a square sail.
GALLEY	The area for food preparation on a ship.
GASKET	A length of line or narrow strip of fabric used to tie a stowed sail in place. The modern term is "sail tie."
GOOSENECK	The fitting that attaches the boom to the mast, allowing the boom to swing.
HALYARD	A line used for raising and lowering a sail.
INBOARD	Toward the centerline of a ship.
IN IRONS	Unable to maneuver because the boat has lost forward momentum.
JIB	A triangular sail that extends from the top of the mast to the bow.
JUMBO	A triangular sail that sets just forward of the foremast.

LAZARETTE — A storage locker used for gear needed on deck, usually near the stern.

LAZY JACKS — A network of lines attached to the mast and to a series of points on either side of the boom that help control the sail when it is lowered.

LIFELINE — A wire running along the outboard edge of a vessel that prevents people from falling overboard.

LINE — A length of rope or other material serving a particular purpose.

LOBSTER POT — A small color-coded float that marks the location of a lobster trap on the bottom.

LOWERS — The four lowest sails on a schooner, which are easily set and managed by a small crew.

MAINSAIL — The principal sail set on the mainmast, the aftermost mast on a schooner.

MAINSHEET — A line that controls the trim of the mainsail.

MAST — A long pole or vertical spar rising from the keel or deck of a boat.

NUN — An unlighted, pointy-topped red buoy that is left on the starboard (right hand) side when returning to harbor.

PAINTER — A line attached to the bow of a small boat, used to tie up to a dock or another vessel.

PINRAIL — A railing with holes to accept belaying pins.

PORT — The left side of a boat when looking forward.

RUDDER — A flat piece, traditionally built of wood, hinged vertically near the stern of a ship and used for steering.

RUST BUST	To remove rust stains in preparation for painting.
SCHOONER	A two-masted ship with the shorter mast forward, historically used for carrying cargo. Most schooners still in use today take passengers for tours.
SKIFF	An open boat with a sharp bow and square stern.
SNUBBER	A short line that takes the strain off the anchor chain while anchored, acting as a shock absorber and silencer.
SPAR	Any of the long poles (mast, boom, gaff) that support sails. Aluminum replaced wood as the standard building material in the middle of the twentieth century.
STARBOARD	The right side of a boat when looking forward.
STERN	The rear end of a boat.
THWART	A seat extending across a boat.
TRANSOM	The flat surface that forms the stern of a square-ended boat.
WINDLASS	A type of winch used especially on ships to hoist anchors.

My father took this photo from the cockpit of the family boat during Hurricane Carol in Hadley's Harbor. I'd always assumed that the vessel was heeling because she had washed ashore, the inspiration for the fictional "Starlight." I have since discovered that she was actually heeled over only from the wind—though she very nearly washed up onto Bull Island shortly after the photo was taken.   -*CNC*

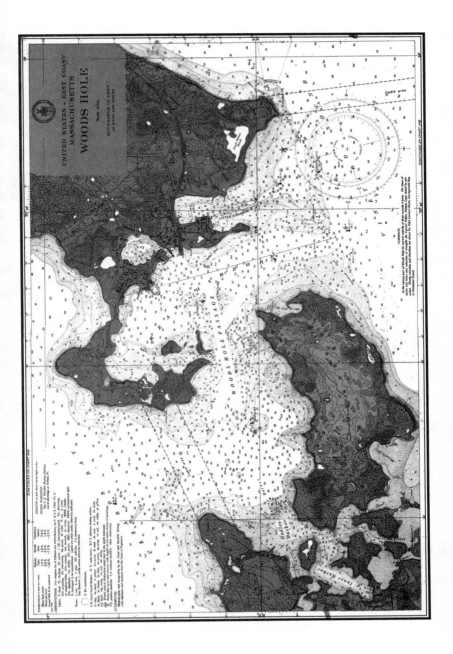

About the Author

Carol Newman Cronin has sailed and written fiction since she was a child. In 2004, she crowned a lifetime of competitive achievement by winning two races for the USA at the Olympics in Athens. A member of the elite US Sailing Team from 2001–2007, she has won numerous national and international sailing championships. Since retiring from Olympic sailing, Carol has focused on writing and graphic design from her home office in Jamestown, RI. *Oliver's Surprise*, her first book, was published in 2008. She and her videographer husband spend as many hours as possible on the water, mostly aboard a Herreshoff Marlin built in 1938.

About the Illustrator

Laurie Ann Cronin grew up on the Hudson River, sailing an old wooden family-owned nineteen foot Rocket that sealed a lifelong love of the water. A graduate of Syracuse University with a degree in painting, Laurie is currently an Art Director/Designer and lives with her husband and son. She visits the water as often as possible, on the nearby Finger Lakes or farther afield in the salty waters of Narragansett Bay.